SPIDER'S RIFT

Book 4 in the Detective Trann series

Christa Yelich-Koth

Look for other books by Christa Yelich-Koth

www.ChristaYelichKoth.com

The Detective Trann series
SPIDER'S TRUTH
SPIDER'S RING
SPIDER'S QUEEN
SPIDER'S RIFT
SPIDER'S LIE

**The Land of Iyah trilogy
(YA fantasy)**
THE JADE CASTLE
THE JADE ARCH
THE JADE THRONE

**Eomix Galaxy Novels
(Sci-fi/fantasy)**
ILLUSION (Book 1 of 2)
IDENTITY (Book 2 of 2)
COILED VENGEANCE

**Graphic Novels
(Sci-fi)**
HOLLOW

**Comic Books
(Sci-fi)**
HOLLOW'S PRSIM SERIES
(6 issues total)
Issue #1: *Aftermath*
Issue #2: *Reunion*
Issue #3: *Alliance*
Issue #4: *Trigger*
Issue #5: *Revelations*
Issue #6: *Fusion*

SPECIAL THANKS

To you, the reader: THANK YOU for wanting more from this series.

Sandra Yelich: What the *what*? How many days do we have left? Thank you as always for your amazing edits.

Conrad Teves: For your fantastic help with the cover art.

Thomas Koth: For beta reading so quickly and loving the avalanche becoming a falling mountain.

1

6 days earlier

Mae skidded across a few rocks in the dirty alleyway, using her hands to hold herself steady, and failing, causing her to slide on her knees.

"Shit, shit, SHIT!" Gaining her balance, she wrapped her fingertips over the edge of the brick building and swung herself around the corner. Slamming her back against the wall, she gulped in breaths. Blood slowly trickled from her scraped palms and knees. Black tights may have looked cute under her plaid skirt, but they provided no protection against a gravelly surface.

A haze had formed in the pre-night sky, giving her some cover, but she worried she'd been seen anyway.

This wasn't the intel, she thought, shaking her head. *No one was supposed to recognize me.*

Half an hour ago, before her current and pathetic attempt to avoid further detection from onlookers, the man had approached her in the alley behind the restaurant. The brisk air bit into her exposed cheeks. She'd just wanted to grab a bite to eat. At 9 p.m., she knew of one restaurant close to the apartment where she lived that would still be open: Lolita Back Bay.

Well, she *sort of* lived in that apartment. The version created by the Triads of herself, called Mags, lived there with her fiancé. But he hadn't been home so she figured going out for food would be all right. Lately she'd been waking up more frequently as herself. Her group, the Coalition, was weaning her off her fake persona. Mags may eventually find out, but the transformation only lasted about a week, so there wasn't much Mags could do except notice "blackout periods." By the time she reported it to a doctor, in which they usually employed the "wait and see if it happens again" method of medicine, Mae would have transitioned to her true self and Mags would be gone.

But now, someone recognized her as her alternate persona.

"What the hell are you doing here, Mags?" the man at the end of the alley yelled, approaching.

She sighed. Normally she could figure out a way to deal with the person, at least enough to get out of the situation, but this guy had screamed in her face. She didn't do well with being disrespected. And she hated the idea that the "other" version of herself would let someone talk to her like this. It made her even more angry at this jerk.

Then she recognized him—Scott. Mags' fiancé. Obviously, they'd had a fight.

Edginess stole over her, and she shot back, "What are YOU doing here?"

A sneer crossed his face. "Not that it's any of your business, but I'm heading to my car. I parked across from the restaurant, in case you wanted to talk. Clearly *that* didn't happen."

Mae paused. "Maybe I changed my mind."

A furrowed brow. "You didn't know I where my car was."

Shit. "I thought you mentioned it."

His eyes narrowed. "You know what, I don't care anymore. Too many times you've said or done weird stuff that you can't explain. You're not my problem anymore." He took a step forward. "You're pathetic, Mags. A waste of a life."

Rage surged inside her, so strongly her vision tunneled for a moment. Fake or not, how *dare* he speak to her that way.

"Hey, Scott!" she called out.

Scott turned around. Mae pulled out her favorite knife, the one she always carried, and plunged it into his gut. A splash of blood spurted onto her hand, warm and sticky. With a slow descent, the body crumbled to the ground.

Mae stood over the now corpse, wiping the blade off on the inside of her jacket. A sniff.

What the...? Three drops of blood dripped from her nose onto Scott's face. *Shit.* Moving to wipe them off, she stopped when she noticed a couple walking past the alleyway.

No time. She hoofed it down the alley in the other direction, skidding on the oil-slicked ground at the end, and found herself now catching her breath.

Her Triad instincts kicked in. She replayed the scene in her head. No, the couple couldn't have seen her.

But the blood on Scott's face…

Nothing I can do right now. I'll report it to my boss. She'll take care of it, I'm sure…

October 17ᵗʰ
6:00 a.m.

Mags' eyes snapped open, and she drew in a shuddering breath. The nightmare she'd just had had been so vivid. Except she didn't remembering killing Scott. At least, not as herself.

Then she recalled. It wasn't a dream. Her alter-ego self had killed Scott in an alley. This had been a memory, just not hers.

About two seconds later Mags realized something else almost as horrific.

She wasn't alone in bed…

Mags held her breath, worried any movement may cause the body attached to the arm draped over her to move. Too much hair on the skin to be Scott.

Besides, Scott was dead.

Eventually, the need for oxygen won out, and she forced herself to breathe as normally as possible, contrary to the racing of her heart.

Okay. Think. Where are you?

A nightstand with a clock on it sat next to her. Six a.m. A curtained window, cracked a few inches, revealed a streetlight outside. Darkness loomed out there, tinged with a low glow of light from the beginnings of a sunrise. A bed that wasn't her own, an arm from someone she didn't recognize.

A hotel. I am in a hotel. But how long ago was that? It could have been days. She thought about the arm around her. *And last time I was me I was* definitely *alone.*

Reality clawed at her mind like an angry cat. Denial wouldn't work anymore. This represented her new situation now. She wasn't real. Merely a construct created by a Triad to cover up the true killer beneath.

But right now, real or not, I'm in control. She wasn't sure how, but she knew she had to take advantage of this time for as long as it lasted. Ever since the MRI when she'd seen the first flashes of her counterpart's memories, she'd been having less and less time as herself. The last instance she remembered...she'd been in a hotel room as well, learning about the APB out on her for murdering Detective Juliette Tay.

Mags thought she might throw up at the memory. Her closest friend....

Why couldn't this all just be a bad dream? she pleaded into the universe. But the clock changed, moving forward, and ignoring her prayer.

Holding her breath once again, Mags slid ever so slowly from under the embrace encircling her. The owner let out a sigh but didn't wake.

Chilled, since she currently wore nothing, Mags wrapped her own arms around her body, shivering. Using the minimal light from the clock, she groped around the nightstand, feeling over its contents.

Glasses. She placed these on her face.

Pen. Not really needed right now.

And here. Phone. Curling her fingers around the device,

she stood and tiptoed to the bathroom. Quietly opening then shutting the door, she turned on the overhead light, which blared too brightly for her tired eyes.

Glancing at the phone through a bleary gaze, she stared at the date. Thursday, October 17th. About 16 hours had passed since her last lucid moments as herself. However, it looked as though she'd missed the meeting from the previous night of...the Coalition, yes, that's what they called themselves.

Okay, who to call. This had been her prior problem. But then she remembered she'd decided to call Sean, as he'd seen his ex-fiancé, Angellica, change into her alternate Triad form. If anyone would believe her, it would be him.

I wish I could call Juliette. She would have believed me. I *just needed more time to convince her...*

A shot of grief pierced her at the memory that Juliette no longer lived.

Because of me.

Except it hadn't been her. Not really. It had been Mae. And yet, if Mags as herself wasn't real, then there was no *her* at all to blame.

The concept made her head swim, and a streak of pain lanced her mind.

Oh no! She remembered now. Her migraines. They caused her to black out, to become her alternate persona once more. She was running out of time.

I can't let the other me know I can be self-aware, she thought. *I have to plan this carefully. Keep stress levels down. Make sure I return myself to where I woke up so she can't tell I've existed. But first, gather intel and send it to Sean.*

Another pulse of pain in her brain. Time was almost up.

Mags hit the button on the phone so she could make a phone call.

Oh crap.

The phone was locked. It wasn't her phone, it was Mae's. And it needed a passcode.

Okay, phone call is out. What other way can I contact him? Email. A computer. She had a laptop last time.

Mags opened the door a sliver to allow light to enter the room. There. On the desk. The laptop.

A third pang of pain.

It's still okay. I have time. I have to have time.

Moving briskly but silently, Mags cracked the door to the bathroom, crossed the room, and opened the laptop away from the bed. Also password protected. She closed it and placed it back onto the table.

Damn. Think, think. You're a fricking computer genius. You just have to get access to any other computer.

Glancing around, Mags noticed a small pop-up piece of cardboard from the hotel on the desk. She brought it near the bathroom light. It read: "Amenities." Included on the list was "Business Center—open 5am-9pm, M-F."

That was it. Next time she took over as herself, she'd go to the Business Center.

Content in her plan, the pain in her head receded slightly as her anxiety and stress diminished. But then the person in the bed rolled over and a shot of fear—and pain—bolted through her.

"You're up?" the man in the bed called out.

"Bathroom," Mags muttered, turning off the bathroom light. Panic constricted her chest and she stood frozen in fear. What if he wanted her to return to bed?

"M'kay," he muttered, turning all the way over, and going silent. A few moments later his breathing became slow and regular.

Apparently, though, the stress of the situation proved too much. A sharp pang lanced through her skull, and she almost fell over. With stumbling steps, Mags made her way over to the bed, crawled in next to the man—while still maintaining a bit of distance between them—and returned the phone to the nightstand.

Before darkness overtook her, the phone lit up with a message.

All she could read through her blurred vision were the following words as part of the message popped up:

"Next target. Short window. Will message when ready. Go to..."

Horror slipped into her mind as she was sucked into nothingness.

Another target.

Someone else was going to die.

2

October 17th
6:15 a.m.

*"My heart belonged to you that night...it still does...I am
the Messiah..."*

The words echoed in Sean's mind through the foggy haze
of being half awake.

The previous night had been one of the worst of his life.
He'd listened to the words in Charlotte's voicemail repeatedly
until they'd been seared into his brain. He'd then driven to her
apartment, but no answer accompanied his frantic buzzing of
the intercom. All phone calls went straight to message, as if her
phone were either dead or turned off.

He'd thought about finding the landlord, ordering him or

her to let Sean check Charlotte's apartment, but how could he? He didn't have a warrant. He didn't have a plausible reason. And claiming that she may be in danger because of some super secret Triads sects wouldn't exactly go over well.

Defeated, he'd driven home, his mind full of swirling thoughts. Coupling that with the four-second message Elaine had sent him of Charlotte claiming she was the Triad Messiah, Sean's alcohol induced, sleep-punctuated night had been filled with nightmares of either Charlotte dying in horrible ways by the hands of Triad members or laughing at him as she sat atop a throne, surrounded by murderous women, waiting to follow her exact orders.

Now, with a cricked neck, he grudgingly moved from his couch to the bathroom to relieve himself. Once the pressure dissipated, he washed his hands in the sink while bloodshot eyes reflected back at him in the mirror.

What am I supposed to do? he thought at his own face.

No answer came.

Options flooded through his mind as he methodically turned on the water to shower. Once hot enough, he stripped out of his T-shirt and boxers and stood under the cleansing wetness.

I have to make a decision, he thought, rubbing soap across his chest. *But what? Do I tell someone about the audio clip and Charlotte's voice? But who should I tell? Elaine, so she can investigate more as a reporter? Inspector Woods from Interpol so he can add Charlotte to some sort of "most wanted" list? Sergeant Millan, who wants nothing more than to retire next week?*

The "who" wasn't the only issue, but "what would happen next?" vied for attention in his turbulent mind.

If he told *anyone*, Charlotte would become a target.

But should she be?

What was she THINKING*?*

Finishing up, he turned off the water, and toweled himself dry. *That* question seemed to matter to him the most. He wanted to know *why* she'd do something like this. The Charlotte he'd gotten to know wanted nothing more than to stop the Triads. So why join them? And not only join them, but claim herself as their leader? He remembered her saying she'd been flattered by the idea of being their "Messiah," so was this a delusion of grandeur? Or maybe someone was forcing her to make the claim? Or had it been because she wanted to instigate change from inside the Triads and chose to play some sort of undercover role?

Her voicemail message to him indicated she'd made the choice to work with these women to help. But how and to what end?

Dressing for the day, Sean glanced once more at his own reflection. *There* has *to be a good reason.* Except nothing made sense anymore. Was there a good explanation for why Mags had become a killer? Or Juliette's death? Or why arsonists were targeting possible Triad agents?

Gripping the edge of the sink, Sean peered into the mirror at his own eyes. Regardless of the lack of answers, only one track would allow him to find any at all.

Do what you do best.

What he did best was being a damn good detective.

There'd been a reason he'd been sought after when he'd left his previous precinct in Philly—his closure rate soared above others in his department. As of now, he was in the dark. But no more. He'd uncover every detail he could, then choose his next path. This would provide the only way to know for sure he'd be doing the right thing. Going to any of the individuals on his list without proof wouldn't work.

First things first—deal with work. The situation there had become tense enough without the distraction of Triads muddling his mind. Except, how could he concentrate on his job when he knew the truth? His job entailed tracking down Mags, who'd been accused of killing not only Detective Tay, but also her ex-fiancé, *and* was involved in the Triads. At least according to Inspector Woods. Except no other officer knew about that last little nugget of information.

In the meantime, he'd just get through the day. That night he could chat with Elaine or Woods, come up with a plan, and move forward.

As for the knowledge that he recognized Charlotte's voice in the audio clip… no need to tell either of them. Yet. Not until he could prove it.

Determined, and content once more to have some focus, Sean finished getting ready for work.

Before he left his apartment, the phone rang. Turning around, Sean answered the landline.

"Hello?"

"Good, I caught you before you left." Sean recognized his partner's voice. He'd been worried about Payne since he'd stormed out of the precinct the day before after Sean had told him about Mags killing Juliette.

"What's going on?"

A short silence. "I think I found Mags."

3

October 17th
6:30 a.m.

Charlotte's eyes slowly opened into the dimness. She'd been dreaming—an insane dream about proclaiming herself the Messiah of the Triads, about Juliette being killed by Mags, who was secretly a Triad agent, and that she'd gone on the run, ready to lead the Triads to a "new" way of living, which meant exposing them so she and the others in her group could track them down and stop them.

The ridiculousness of the dream made her smile, which then slowly slid off her face as reality sunk in.

All of it was real.

The familiar sense of tightness in her chest as anxiety crept in forced her to exhale strongly, as if she could expel the horrible feelings inside her. But the past few weeks had been an indication that the best thing for her to do when anxiety hit was to distract herself. With measured movements, she wiggled herself off the top bunk of the RV and made her way to its small bathroom.

She began with a check of all her injured areas, as best she could. The bruise on her elbow from having dashed out of a hotel window after the main room exploded was now a greenish-brown—healing, but still appearing quite hideous. The stitches on her back felt all right; she couldn't quite see them in the mirror, but Carla, who'd inspected them the night before, told her they were healing well. The slash above her eyebrow from when Violet had smashed her face into a car door appeared almost gone—just a sliver of paler skin remained, cutting a little into the eyebrow line.

Even though she'd put so much effort into keeping up her appearance over the years, a sense of satisfaction at the scars on her body surprised her. With the whole theory of "perfection" by the Triads, so strong they'd kill people over it, Charlotte liked the idea of being a bit imperfect.

Once ready for the day, her anxiety having dissipated while she counted toothbrush strokes, she crossed over to the main living area, noting on her way that the bottom bunk lay empty, and the bed made. That meant Isabella must be either driving or gone. A lack of rumbling beneath her feet eliminated the first option.

She'd almost gotten used to the idea of this place as her current residence. Even though the camper didn't stay in the same location for very long, it remained the place she'd inhabited the longest amount of time so far since she'd first fled with Isabella five days ago. Meaning she'd stayed in the RV more than one night, so it felt "familiar."

A whisper of a laugh passed through her lips. Had it only been five days since she'd gone to the lake house to confront the woman who'd killed her brother so many years ago? Only to have the woman, who was a Triad third, attack her, almost kill her, and end up dead instead by Charlotte's hand.

It was self-defense, she reminded herself.

Still, it had changed her. In between dreams about Triad women worshipping her and fantasies of returning home and snuggling up on the couch with Sean came images of that woman's face, pale and lifeless. Though she didn't consider herself a murderer, she was now more like these women than not.

At that thought, the door to the RV swung open and Isabella entered, carrying two paper bags full of items.

"Morning," she said, noticing Charlotte.

Charlotte hurried over to help, taking one of the bags, and placing it on the table. A fresh, cool breeze wafted through the small space from the open door and Charlotte took in a deep breath. More than anything, it helped soothe her anxiety to get some openness in the cramped area.

"Good morning," she replied. "Supplies?"

Isabella nodded, her cheeks rosy from the brisk air. "I'm not sure how many more times we'll be able to go out in public for the next several days, so I wanted to make sure we would be all right during that time." She began to unpack the bags. "How did you sleep?"

Charlotte thought about it. Though full of dreams, she'd slept soundly through the night, a change from most of the nights this past week. "Surprisingly...well."

Isabella paused for a moment. "I assumed you'd have trouble, because of everything that took place yesterday. Claiming yourself Messiah and broadcasting it to the other Triads is no small thing."

"I had a lot of dreams, but apparently my body was too tired to put up a hefty fight." Charlotte thought about her panic this morning after reality set in. "I suppose my mind made me believe everything had been a dream, a dream too surreal to even be a nightmare, but it was not."

Isabella briefly touched Charlotte's arm. "I know we didn't get to talk much yesterday after your declaration. It was a big step. I don't want you to think I don't realize that." Isabella stuck the last flashlights and double sets of batteries in a drawer.

"I am not sure what I would say even if we *did* talk about it. I fear my whole life the past few days has been a churning mess of 'too much too quickly.' Adding last night's recording to the mix...? I have not really processed anything yet."

Isabella paused, her face contemplative. "I get it. I felt the same way after the bomb went off in my apartment and my girlfriend was murdered." Though Isabella seemed to be all right, Charlotte heard the small catch in her words. "Truth is, within the same twenty-four hours of her death, a reporter and an officer I worked with were also killed. It was as though...I went through the motions of dealing with the logistics, reporting the death and the like, but I didn't really remember what I'd done that day. All I knew was it was the first time I'd ever told anyone about the Triads and within a day, both these other people were dead. I sort of…blurred through it until I was able to think again."

Charlotte nodded in understanding. "That is how last night felt. A blur. I know that after I recorded the speech we went over our next steps and I read more from the Book, or at least my gaze followed words, but I did not absorb any of it."

Isabella smiled. "Well, for right now, until we send out our follow-up message, we should be safe. What do you think about taking a jog around the campgrounds with me? It's still dark enough and quiet. Plus, it may be a while before we get to stretch our legs that much again."

Charlotte glanced around their tight surroundings. "A jog sounds like an excellent idea."

While tying her running shoes—a new addition to her "on the go" wardrobe, Charlotte watched Isabella send a message to Carla about their plan for the day.

"It must be exhausting," Charlotte noted.

"What is?"

"To constantly be running and looking over your shoulder."

Isabella finished her message and pocketed the phone. "I guess I don't think about it much anymore. It's just…how I live. It's a routine now."

Charlotte stood. "Do you ever worry about complacency?"

"That's what I have Carla for," Isabella said with a smile. "She never relaxes and always keeps us on our toes. I think it's why we haven't lost anyone else since she and I teamed up."

A sense of relief unexpectedly washed over Charlotte. These women may live dangerous lives, but they looked out for each other, made sure they all remained safe. And though she and Carla hadn't originally gotten off on the best of terms, once it was established that Carla believed Charlotte to be the Messiah, the dynamic shifted between the two of them. No matter how she felt about the situation, Charlotte knew Carla would keep her safe. She was one of them.

The notion spiked a momentary jolt of electricity in her spine.

She was one of them.

Shaking off the notion, Charlotte followed Isabella out of the RV and they started their jog. Sunlight began to lighten their surroundings. A myriad of autumn colors swayed around them as sharp winds cut through the trees. The chill nipped at her nose and puffs of foggy air formed in front of her mouth when she exhaled. Though only mid-October, she wondered if snow would come early this year with the dropping temperatures.

Charlotte mentally laughed. The benign nature of her thoughts, with everything else she should be thinking about, amused her. And yet, this felt like perhaps one of the last times in a long while she would be able to push everything aside, give her brain a break.

After about an hour, with chilled cheeks and earlobes, the two women slowed to walk the last few hundred yards.

"I haven't been able to run like that in a long time," Isabella said, unzipping the front of her fleece jacket.

"Me either." Though cold at first, gratefulness at her

thinner jacket washed over her. The only thing she regretted was not wearing a hat. "I used to run in high school, but once college started, I switched to volleyball, continuing on from my junior and senior years in high school, and running became part of the exercise program. I stopped doing it because I enjoyed it and only kept up with running because it was required."

"I never liked running, not until I trained for my Triad position."

Charlotte waited a beat. "Why did you join?" She'd been curious for quite some time, but never knew if she had the right to ask. Now, as part of their group, she felt like no topic would be out of bounds.

"Looking back, it seems like a different life. I suppose, in a way, it was." Isabella rubbed her nose. "There is a passage in the Book which discusses how Triad members are picked. There has been some...debate...about a few of the word choices."

"In translations, there usually are."

Isabella nodded. "The two main translations used define the type of Triad a person joins. The first option is, 'The most humane will judge, the most clever will plan, and the most zealous will remove.' That is the one my Triad followed. As far as I know, almost all of them follow that translation."

Charlotte thought about the words. They made sense. Except there was a little leeway. "Remove. You mean kill."

Isabella cleared her throat in agreement.

"But 'remove' could mean something else besides death. Couldn't it?" Charlotte suggested.

"Any reference to the word always spoke of removing from civilization, removing from the community, removing from the world. With the context around it in other parts of the Book, some people translated it as 'kill.'"

"I assume that is part of the alternate translation?"

Isabella nodded. "'The most kind will judge, the most wise will plan, the most impassioned will kill.'"

Charlotte thought about the differences. They did seem fairly similar: humane and kind, clever and wise, remove and kill. And yet, as an academic, she understood how important translations could be. Context, of course, was critical, but the period of time the writing came from also mattered. People wrote based on their own experiences, their own current knowledge. As the world evolved, the translations were often skewed to fit the new society, instead of updated and changed.

Charlotte connected the interpretations with Isabella's position. "So that is why you were chosen to be a primary—you were deemed humane?"

"Yes."

"Humane does not sound too bad."

Isabella laughed. "But what you forget is that their definition of 'humane' means we look at humanity as a whole in order to cull them. For the greater good is considered 'humane.'"

Charlotte let out a sharp breath. "It sounds very callous."

"It was."

Charlotte gave Isabella a sharp look. Though thorough, she didn't picture Isabella as callous. "That does not match up with what I know of you now, which returns me to my question. Why did you join?"

"At the time, I was...disillusioned with life. I worked in a research lab studying behavioral patterns of humans for the sociology department. Day after day of watching the horribleness of humanity sunk into my bones. I was bullied as a child, due to the fact I was born with rosacea, and it didn't clear up until I was about five or so. But I remember the cruelness of my peers and it made me question human behavior."

Charlotte could relate, seeing as how she'd been made fun of for her birthmark, which also eventually faded. The harshness of those children's words while growing up shaped her social life, creating isolation and a determination to always appear healthy and fault-free. "That definitely makes you sound like the perfect candidate to join a Triad."

"I told you, they are thorough." She kicked away a broken branch from the pathway and rubbed her nose again. "I thought I could help improve humanity, change it. It's what I'd always wanted to do. I grew up surrounded by the dead—my parents owned a mortuary—so I'd never been afraid of death. But it didn't allow me to connect to the point of life or understand why humans respond the way they do. That's why I got into sociology, to figure out the *why*. Except studies didn't provide me any answers. My comfortableness with death and my constant need to question everything put me at odds with most of my peers."

"Which made you, once again, a perfect candidate to join with a tight-knit group of like-minded women."

"And a way to help the world. Or so I thought."

"Well, if you had not joined, you would never have gotten the opportunity to stop the Triads either. And that *will* change the world."

Isabella gave a soft smile. Then she sniffed and rubbed her nose a third time. "Ugh," she muttered, "something is tickling my nose."

"Allergies?"

"No, it's more like..." She trailed off as they rounded the final bend in the campsite road, revealing their RV a few hundred feet away.

Engulfed in flames.

4

October 17th
7:45 a.m.

Sean pulled into the precinct's parking lot and found a spot, his heart racing. He noticed Payne waiting for him, leaning against his own vehicle, a black pick-up truck. Once parked, Sean exited his Jag and walked over. The man looked pretty good, considering he'd been bashed over the head and had surgery on his brain a week ago. Ironically enough saving the very woman the entire Boston police force currently sought.

Could his partner really have seen Mags? If so, what would that mean? She had to be brought in, to face charges for murdering Juliette, but Interpol wanted to speak with her first in connection to the Triad arsonists. And Sean wanted to speak to her as well. Maybe, if she *was* linked to the Triads, she'd have some information about Charlotte's involvement. But how could he find her, speak to her, bring her to Interpol, and then turn her in without her revealing all those interrogations to the police?

Sean cleared his mind and approached the truck. "Morning, Payne."

"Trann." Payne cleared his throat. "I'll get right to it. I know you gotta head into work." The slowed speech from a few days ago had disappeared and Payne sounded like his normal Texan self.

Sean glanced over at the building beside them. A place which usually filled him with purpose and pride, now merely a distraction so he didn't have to think about Triad stuff for a while. "You possibly seeing Mags *is* work. Technically."

Payne scowled. "You promised, man."

Their conversation that morning, though brief, had ended with Sean swearing he wouldn't tell anyone at the precinct about what Payne believed he saw. And, technically, this current conversation held a much less volatile atmosphere than the last time they'd spoken in person—when Sean had informed Payne about Mags' involvement with Juliette's death. The large man had gone berserk, knocking over a chair, and denying that the situation could be possible before stalking out of the break room.

Now, Sean held his hands up, defensive, recalling the end of their phone call that morning. "Don't worry. I didn't tell anyone. Yet. But if you really know where she is..."

"I said I *think*."

"Okay. Just...tell me what you think you saw."

Payne shifted his stance. He stood up straighter, his feet planted firmly. Sean recognized the position. Payne was one of the best detectives Sean had ever worked with. In the field, he was no-nonsense and spot on with his protocols. The stance indicated that Payne was in what Sean liked to call "work mode." Which, to Sean, meant Payne was very serious about what he saw.

"I want to remind you first that I'm not fully back on duty until Monday, so this is coming from a civilian."

Sean crossed his arms. "Payne. Talk."

"I was traveling west on Beacon. Right before the junction to highway ninety, I saw a woman fitting the description of Mags traveling eastbound. She was driving a white Taurus. Partial license beginning XU."

"Why didn't you report it?"

"I did. I called you right away. It happened this morning." Payne's body shifted once more to a more neutral position. "Trann, I don't know what's going on. I can't believe Mags had anything to do with Juliette's death. I thought, based on what you described, maybe she'd been hurt or kidnapped and someone else killed Tay. But seeing her driving this morning...apparently fine..." Payne hung his head.

Sean understood the defeat behind that movement. "I get it," Sean said. "None of us want to believe Mags could have done this. And truth is, we won't know anything for sure until she's brought in. If she's mixed up in something or in over her head, you know the best way to help her is to find her." He slapped a hand on Payne's shoulder. "Let's go inside and I'll take your full statement."

As they moved through the entrance, Payne mumbled something.

"What?" Trann asked over the hustle of the morning officers. Nothing had been quiet at the station since the APB had been sent out for Mags the day before.

"Maybe I wanted it to be her, who I saw," Payne repeated more loudly.

The two of them entered their shared office. Sean took a seat behind his desk while Payne remained standing, pacing, actually, like a caged animal.

"You want to sit?"

Payne shook his head. "It doesn't make sense, Trann. Why would she do this? And why would I...?" He trailed off, a look of both hurt and confusion on his face.

Sean understood. "Why would you have fallen for her?" He'd felt the same way when he'd learned his ex, Angellica, was a killer.

No more movement. Payne gazed through the windows out onto the bullpen, his eyes a tad glassy. "I've never been hooked on a girl like this before. I was even engaged once, in Texas, but after a few months, she got all bride-crazy and I had to dump her bitchy ass." He cleared his throat. "Sorry."

Sean knew the transition Payne had made from sexist asshole to being a better man would take some time and he waved away the crass comments. And yet, the reason for the change had been because of Mags. If she really ended up being guilty, would Payne revert to his old patterns?

Sean proceeded slowly. "Like you said, we don't have all the facts. That's why we have to find her." He still didn't know exactly what he wanted to do *if* he found her. The choice between following protocol and discovering the truth seemed to be growing blurrier by the second.

"I don't know where she was going."

"No, but this is the first real lead we've had so far. A car and a partial plate. We can see if it progresses anywhere."

Payne hesitated, then gave a curt nod. "I know that procedure doesn't always work perfectly, but no matter what's going on with her, if she did it or if she's just caught up in something, we gotta find her." He rubbed his beard stubble. "I want to help. I *need* to help."

"I know. But you can't get involved, not officially, until you're reinstated."

Payne gripped the edges of the desk. "I can't just sit at home. Could you? If it was someone you cared about?"

Sean thought of Charlotte. He had to admit, even after Payne had called, part of him still wanted to drive to her place again and see if she was home, even though he knew she wouldn't be there. Mags needed to be a priority. And yet...if he knew where Charlotte might be, he would absolutely drop everything to find her.

"I get it," Sean said quietly. "I completely get it." He paused. "Listen, I'll fill you in the best I can, off the record."

"That's not enough," Payne growled.

"It'll have to be. There are...too many players involved already. We've got Tay's cases to reassign, everyone here is running around like they've lost their minds, and you know we're going to be under constant scrutiny. Reporters are every-where, citizens are rearing their heads again, calling us incompetent for letting something like this happen."

"You think Internal Affairs will get involved?"

Sean's forehead furrowed. "I'm not sure. Depends on if someone claims we dropped the ball somehow. I mean, a police department employee killing a detective and then going on the run? If they smell corruption, they'll have their noses in everything." *Which will make things that much harder for me to keep what I know under wraps as well.*

At that moment, Detective Wilt stuck his head in. His receding hairline looked oilier than usual and the bags under his eyes showed he probably hadn't slept on top of not showering. "Hey. Oh, hey Payne. You working again already?"

"Not until Monday," Payne muttered.

"Well, glad to see you up and about." The words held no real emotion behind them. Sean wasn't surprised. Wilt had not only lost a partner, but a friend.

Wilt nodded at Sean, his eyes bleary. "Meeting. Millan's office. Five minutes."

"Be right there," Sean said. After Wilt left, Sean quickly took down everything Payne saw.

"You promise you'll let me know if you find her?" Payne asked.

"I swear."

Payne gave another sharp nod and left.

Sean made his way to Millan's office. The only other people inside were Wilt and Millan.

"Close the door," Millan said once Sean entered.

Wilt glanced at the sergeant, his forehead furrowed. "I thought this was a meeting?"

"It is. But just for the three of us. Sit."

Sean and Wilt settled into the chairs opposite their boss. The wood creaked beneath them. A crisp wisp of air circled in from the narrowly opened window behind Millan. Scents of dried leaves and a tang of coldness hit him and he wondered briefly if they'd get snow early this year.

"You two are the only ones who know I'm retiring. I want to keep it that way until I make the announcement on Monday."

They both nodded.

"However, that's not why you're here this morning. I'm sure you've both guessed by now that our precinct is a laughingstock. An employee under our noses killed one of our own. There's talk of bringing in an outside task force to take over the search for Mags."

Wilt frowned. "That's not right. These are our people. This is up to us to fix this. And it *just* happened two days ago."

Millan coughed and when he continued, his voice sounded a tad hoarser. "Doesn't matter what we think. I heard from the Chief of Police this morning. This is too messy, especially occurring so soon after Veronica Chassis' escape from police custody."

Wilt's voice rose, the heat evident in his words. "What? There's no way that crazy woman's escape and what happened with Mags is related. We don't even *know* what went on between Mags and Tay."

Sean stayed silent, his gut a tight ball. If Mags *was* connected to the Triads, *could* she have helped Violet escape? Or even worse, had she somehow been involved in Violet's death? It had been ruled a mugging gone wrong, but if these Triad women were determined to tie up loose ends...

"The evidence indicates Mags murdered Tay," Millan said curtly. "And as for Miss Chassis, well we just look bad to everyone: public, newscasters, higherups. They will be investigating into every nook and cranny of how we've been handling things. Hell, as soon as it gets out that I'm retiring, I wouldn't be surprised if people claimed that's the reason I'm stepping down."

"It's still bullshit," Wilt muttered, pulling a toothpick from his shirt pocket and chewing on it. "We've just had bad luck. Those crazy Triad women ruined our lives here, but that doesn't mean we're incompetent because of Mags." He paused and let out a sigh. "Sarge, it's *Mags*...how could she have...?"

Millan went on, ignoring Wilt's lingering question. Sean speculated if his boss wondered about Mags' capability as well or if he just wanted to be done with this whole scenario, from precinct to cases to caring.

"If a task force comes," Millan said, "I want you two to be completely cooperative. They'll be interviewing everyone, taking over any leads. I don't want *any* resistance." He leaned forward, his dark eyes narrowed, and continued. "This is your chance, now, right here, to come clean about *anything* revolving around Mags and Tay's case. Anything you left out of your report."

Wilt immediately shook his head. "No, sir. Everything is square."

"Trann?"

Sean's head swirled with all the secrets he currently kept: his connection with Inspector Woods and Interpol, working with Elaine, hearing Charlotte's voice on the clip, arsonists, and his knowledge that other Triads existed, and that Mags may be entangled with them...

Logically, he knew he should tell his boss everything. That was his job. That was the law.

But he still had no proof. Woods had made it clear he wouldn't corroborate any participation with Sean. Elaine would deny she was working on anything Triad-related, as she feared for her own life and knew making waves would only bring attention to herself. And Charlotte's voice...that could have been anything. Doctored. Recorded and manipulated from her words at the trial. Done under duress.

How could he say anything without proof?

"No, sir," Sean finally replied, swallowing against the lump that had risen from his stomach and now sat lodged in his throat. "There's nothing else to tell you."

5

October 17th
8:00 a.m.

Shock coursed through Charlotte as she stared at the burning mass of metal and rubber in front of her. Acrid smoke stung her eyes. Several people had emerged from their nearby campers to check out the commotion. She turned to Isabella for their next move, but Isabella's eyes had nearly bulged from their sockets.

"All our stuff..." Isabella muttered. "Our provisions. The laptop." Her face lost all its color. "Oh my God, the BOOK!" With a movement as if to leap forward, Isabella began to take off. Charlotte reached out and snatched her backwards, nearly missing the grab on the back of her jacket.

"You cannot," Charlotte hissed.

"But the Book!" Isabella's eyes filled with tears.

A sudden explosion blew apart the RV. Campers scrambled away, shrieking and covering their heads as debris flew all around them. Campground representatives cleared any stragglers from the area, shouting about the approaching fire department.

Charlotte choked on her next words. "It is gone. The Book is gone. Everything is gone." She glanced around, noticing the crowds thickening at a safer distance. The fire wasn't spreading, although some staff were hastily picking up burnt chunks of siding which had flown into a more wooded area. The wind shifted, now coming from behind Charlotte, and the smoke in her eyes cleared a touch. It wouldn't be long until someone noticed them as most of the campers had congregated on the far side. "We have to leave, but we cannot be conspicuous."

Isabella stood there, trembling, with Charlotte's arm now wrapped around her bicep, in case she attempted to dash forward again.

With a shaky breath, Charlotte led the traumatized woman away from the scene. She kept her eyes open for anything conspicuous, but no one seemed to be watching them. Instead, the bystanders' stares were glued to the fire engine that just pulled up. As the two of them rounded the bend and left visual range, Charlotte's last glimpse was of the crowd being pushed further away as a nearby tree caught fire.

The two of them retraced their steps along the trail they'd come, the air suddenly colder. "What is our next move?" Charlotte asked.

Isabella shook her head. "I-I don't know. I can't believe…" The Italian woman stumbled on a root, then grasped Charlotte for support. "Everything…our food, our supplies, the Book…all gone."

A sense of surrealness settled upon Charlotte. Feeling outside herself, she moved through the motions as if someone else directed her. The situation reminded her of being at work. Dealing with someone who'd died, especially in a brutal way, always gave her a moment of pause. But then she sunk into her training and relied on her knowledge and muscle memory to keep moving to get through the situation. "All right. Give me your phone. I will call Carla to fill her in and then enact a plan."

Isabella mechanically handed over her phone.

Charlotte turned it on, its screen glowing to life. Only two numbers were listed in the contact list identified as 2 and 3. Charlotte assumed Isabella used the Triad numbering system in her mind—old habits were hard to break—so she chose number three. Sure enough, after two rings, Carla answered.

"Yes?" she asked, a Spanish lilt tingeing the beginning of the word.

"This is Charlotte."

A tiny pause. "What has happened?"

"The RV. We went for a jog and when we returned, it was on fire."

"*Ay, Dios mio.*" A longer pause. "Are you both okay?"

"Yes. We were not anywhere near the vehicle."

"Anything to salvage?"

Charlotte recalled the blackened metallic mess. "I do not think so." She swallowed. "The Book was inside."

"We will worry about remains after you two get to a safe location. Were you spotted?"

"I do not think so."

"You don't think so or you *know* so?"

Charlotte replayed the scene in her head, pulling on the limited training she'd received during the past few days. "I know we were not spotted."

"Excellent. Exit the campground and take Summer Street east, then Wiggins Ave north. There's a strip mall over there. I'll meet you at the Chipotle. I will be there in...one hour. That's about how long it'll take you to walk there. Drop the phone as soon as you can. I'll fill Jordan in on everything."

"Okay. We will meet you soon." Charlotte hung up, relayed the details to Isabella, and the two of them continued away from the fiery mess behind them. On their way out of the campground, they deleted Isabella's phone info and dropped the item into a large receptacle. Charlotte's burner phone had been in the camper.

Charlotte had never felt so far away from safety in her life. She couldn't go home, she couldn't call for help. All she could do was put one foot in front of the other and hope her destination brought her some sense of comfort.

They moved in silence. Even the wildlife around them had stilled, most likely in response to the smoky air wafting through the trees. About twenty minutes into their walk, Isabella asked one question.

"How could anyone have found us?"

The words hung around them like a tantalizing fog—not quite tangible enough to help them, but just enough to cloud their vision and keep them ill at ease.

"We will figure it out," Charlotte finally said, several minutes later. "You three have come this far without any incident."

"No, we've been lucky. I got my girlfriend killed. Also, a journalist who worked to expose the Triads. Plus, an officer who wanted to help me apprehend these women for their crimes. I survived because I fled Italy and dropped off the Triads' radar. But somehow, I'm in their sights once more. First the hotel, now here?"

"You said they were tracking me at the hotel, not you."

"They were. But you've declared yourself the Messiah. Other Triads *know* you're working with a Triad group. You couldn't have gotten the Book on your own. Or sent out the message without someone's help. Except there is no way to track you anymore. So how? What did we miss?"

Charlotte could hear the desperation in her own voice. "But you three are clever. Just look at some of the things you have accomplished in the past six months. You have thwarted their attempts to kill me, kept me safe, and helped keep those in my life safe as well. However they found you, it may not have been because of you. Perhaps someone saw me?"

"Where? When?" Isabella shook her head and rubbed her arms. The day hadn't gotten much warmer, and they were still dressed for jogging, not sustained time outside. "We may be clever, but there's one thing you're forgetting."

"What is that?"

"These women are just as smart as we are. They've under-gone the same training. And, they have access to more resources we do. Money and technology. Our supplies are limited. And apparently they have an arson group at their disposal."

Charlotte had never thought about those topics. They'd simply always had new supplies, new phones, new technology or rental cars or hotel rooms. "Is there a way to tap into their resources? To add to our own assets?"

Isabella shook her head. "Don't forget, each Triad group is autonomous. They each have their own supply of funding and tricks."

"Where do they get it from?"

"The Book says we are allowed to have 'Money gotten by spilled blood, frozen by the protectors.'"

Charlotte's forehead furrowed. "What does that mean?"

Isabella kicked at a stone. Talking about the Triads and the Book seemed to calm her down a bit. "It means we can steal from corrupt authorities. Or assets frozen by companies, like drug money or stolen goods. Money that could be used for good, but instead remains sealed away by those who think they are above us." She gave a weak laugh. "I would tell you I'll show you the passage in the Book later, but now..."

Charlotte didn't realize how difficult losing the Book would be to Isabella. It was the original edition of basically a religious icon.

"It is still difficult to believe so many women are willing to kill, not to mention steal, lie, and cheat, for one Book written thousands of years ago."

Isabella got very quiet, and Charlotte wondered if she'd offended her. After all, Isabella had chosen to join a Triad as well.

After a few more minutes, as the strip mall came into view, Isabella finally said, "All I know, is, this world is broken. It's out of balance. And the Book not only showed us that, it predicted it. A group of women, a long time ago, realized the trouble the human race was in, long before they could have seen that outcome. They recognized the signs in their own communities." She paused. "It's enticing to feel like you're not alone in these types of thoughts. And more than that, to no longer feel helpless. The Book gave us the chance to regain power, to restructure the world and make it better. To be a part of something larger than ourselves. To feel important, special, and needed. The attraction was very appealing."

Charlotte thought about her own predicament. She, too, was trying to change things on a grander scale. She'd proclaimed herself the Messiah of a group of killers. *But to help stop them,* she thought to herself. And yet, she realized she'd never gotten a straight answer from Isabella or Carla or Jordan about what would transpire if any of the Triad women decided they didn't want to stop murdering. Up until this point, their team simply killed any uncooperative people.

And yet she could see their predicament. These murderers couldn't be brought to justice. There weren't enough resources to monitor them all, to make sure they didn't continue killing. So, what could be the alternative?

Charlotte wasn't sure, but she needed to believe they could do something else besides killing these criminals. Except until she had an alternative solution to offer, what would be her argument?

A stray thought flitted through her mind, but before she

could ask another question, a grey van pulled up next to them on the sidewalk. Pressure on her arm increased as Isabella squeezed it.

"What?" Charlotte whispered.

"Something's not right."

Almost as if those words set things in motion, a second van, this one black, pulled slightly ahead of the two women, squealing its tires as it came to an abrupt stop. Doors opened on both vehicles and four individuals popped out, heading directly for them.

"Run!" Isabella shouted. She gave Charlotte a shove to head her towards the business buildings beside them. Stumbling for a moment, adrenaline coursed through her, and even though the two of them had recently run for an hour, Charlotte felt like she could sprint for days to evade this new threat.

But any thought of escape was crushed as an object smacked her at the ankles, entangling her feet. She tipped forward, arms outstretched, and landed unceremoniously on the frosted grass in front of her. Air rushed from her lungs. Her knees and hands thrummed with pain. The scent of wet grass crept into her nostrils. She could hear rustling behind her as Isabella fought with their would-be captors.

Charlotte brought her feet up to her chest, attempting to dislodge whatever kept her from running, but before she could do more than tug at some sort of metallic threading wrapped around her ankles, two figures approached. Her first instinct was to scream out "Fire!," a tactic she'd once learned in a self-defense class. People tended to call 911 and respond to a situation more often if they thought there was a fire, as opposed to responding to someone yelling "Help!"

But she didn't cry out. If she did, the authorities would come. She couldn't get them involved. Or a nearby citizen would become a target if they witnessed the scene.

In these few moments of thought, her attackers had already bounded over to her. A plastic ball was shoved into her mouth, then covered with duct tape. They lifted her to her feet.

"If you resist," one of them rasped in her ear, "we'll kill her."

At that moment, Charlotte saw a limp Isabella being dragged towards the black van. Her two attackers swiftly moved her—half-carrying her since her ankles were still bound—to the grey van.

Oh God, we have been separated...

Once inside, a black cloth bag swept over her head, obstructing her view. She heard a *beep* and a crackling hiss. Then one of her attackers spoke.

"Package acquired. The other one is now clear for removal. Burn the body."

A walkie talkie, Charlotte thought. Then she realized what the attacker's words meant.

They planned to kill Isabella anyway.

A new sense of fear swept through her. She'd grown accustomed to the fact that, even though dangerous Triad members might be after her, she had the protection of Isabella, Carla, and Jordan to keep her safe.

But now, Isabella would be dead, and Carla and Jordan wouldn't know where she was being taken.

She was on her own.

6

October 17th
5:30 p.m.

Sean's head ached. He waved goodbye to Wilt and left the precinct. The entire day hadn't gone much better than the previous one. Their department was a mess. Phone lines became flooded with calls from reporters and complaints about the lack of ability of the department to take care of their own, as well as with false sightings of Mags all around the city. Or, if the sightings were legit, by the time anyone responded, Mags was nowhere to be found.

The same problem occurred with Payne's intel—even if he had seen Mags driving that morning, she was long gone by the time they checked the highway. And there weren't any traffic cameras to help pick her out and follow the vehicle he'd described. Even the partial license plate had brought up too many options for them to check through.

Sean rubbed his eyes as he got behind the wheel of his Jag. He still had a meeting with Inspector Woods in about an hour. While driving to the office building where they were supposed to meet, Sean filtered through all the notes he'd personally taken *off* the record about his involvement so far with the Triads and what he could do moving forward.

Four points of interest were on his plate: A) Find Mags. B) Find Charlotte. C) Figure out who was setting the fires and why. D) Determine the connection between A and B and C with the Triads.

As a detective, he had three routes he liked to employ to move a stagnant investigation forward: 1) reexamine the evidence, 2) recontact anyone involved, and 3) focus on anyone or any place who *may* have been involved but hadn't come up in the initial investigation. For example, he'd had a case in Philly during which they were tracking a carjacker. They had a description of the thief, but instead of searching at the locations the car thief stole the cars *from,* Sean focused on where they were found once dumped *afterwards.* Each car had been discovered within a mile or so radius of a mini mall. Sean and his team at the time staked out the mall and sure enough, the thief eventually popped into the food court. After they arrested him, they found another car he'd stolen that morning within that same mile radius.

With the Triad situation, he wanted to reexamine the evidence. Except, there wasn't really any. That was the problem.

These women, including Mags and Charlotte, hadn't left much of a trail. And the evidence for the Triad trial had been stolen by someone in a red Jeep that had crashed into Wilt on the first day of the trial. When Sean had requested any traffic camera shots of the crash, it only showed the Jeep speeding away into a suburban area with no other cams, and finally reported as abandoned a week later. There hadn't been any plates on the vehicle and the VIN connected it to a vehicle stolen three months earlier in Maine.

His second step would be to recontact anyone involved, but those involved were either on the run, hiding, or dead.

Except...maybe that wasn't quite true. Sean's mind flittered back to the trial and the few women arrested who'd lived in the bunker with Truth, the leader of the Triad group. He'd talked to them once before, mostly to find out more information about the bunker itself and the movements of that Triad group, but he'd never pressed them about *other* Triads. At the time, he hadn't believed other Triads existed. And, if he recalled correctly, one woman said something about...new recruits? Perhaps they meant for other Triads?

Sean shook his head, unable to precisely remember the conversation. He'd have to contact all the women from the case and revisit them in jail. Perhaps they might know about other Triad groups or how to contact them. If nothing else, maybe they would know something about this "Messiah" figure and what her duties entailed. If so, Sean could track Charlotte based on what she might be accomplishing in that role.

Happy with a plan in mind, he moved to his next dilemma—what to share with Inspector Woods. Sean pulled into the building's lot and parked. He knew he wasn't going to mention the snippet of sound byte he'd heard from Elaine of Charlotte's voice until he knew more information about the circumstances around the recording. But would he be doing a disservice by withholding that piece of information? Woods and his team might have a way to track where that sound clip came from. Although Elaine said she'd found it on a website...

A light went off in his head. If he and Elaine could track down the person who ran that website, they, themselves, could find out about the clip first.

Sean stepped from his car when he noticed Woods coming out the front doors. His shiny, dark head gleamed under the doorway's lights. A brisk breeze fluttered his dark purple dress shirt. Sean thought it odd he hadn't brought a jacket in the evening chill.

"Hey," Sean called out, waving.

Woods gave a nod before lighting up a cigarette. "Detective," he replied, blowing out a puff of smoke. His English accent crisped the word.

"Can't believe I got here on time," Sean said, jogging over. An overwhelming scent of the huge, fat flowers in pots on either side of the entrance, currently dying in the late autumn air, hit him. He felt sure the next decoration on the agenda would be some sort of Christmas-y small trees with fake tinsel and lit up baubles. The idea of Christmas coming in just a couple months shocked him. With so much that had occurred, he hadn't realized how much time had passed. It felt like the end of the year should still be miles away.

The normality of something like a holiday struck him. He

wanted to sit and drink eggnog and open presents and do all the stupid traditions with her. What if he lost her after having just found her?

"I'm surprised you've arrived so promptly as well," Woods said, pulling Sean from his bleak thoughts. "I'm sure the precinct was overrun today. Any progress on the search for Margaret Stinson?"

"Nothing yet. Sightings, but nothing concrete." He rubbed his hands to warm them against the wind. "Anything new with you?"

"Unfortunately, dead ends as well. I delivered the prosthetic ear from Detective Tay to a chap who I thought could help, but he determined that whatever mechanism lay inside the blasted thing had completely burned itself up." He blew out a sharp stream. He offered Sean a cigarette.

"No thanks, I don't smoke," Sean replied.

"I quit years ago. Only started up again once I moved here, though I've kept that secret. This case..." he trailed off.

"I get it." Sean wondered about the tall, dark, British, Interpol inspector. How'd he become involved in all this Triad business in the first place? Woods had put together a team, even moved across the pond, as the Brits might say, to pursue this. And all without official sanction from Interpol. Must be a lonely life. Did he have a significant other? Children back home? Or was he "married to the job?"

From what the inspector had encountered so far, Sean found Woods to be crisp, professional, and, for lack of a better phrase, very put together. The Triads were messy, random, and untraceable. So, what had sparked an interest for Woods that would make him leave his button-down lifestyle?

Whatever the reason, it had to be enough to keep him interested, but rattle him, nonetheless.

Woods stared at the half-smoked cigarette. "It's not actually helping. We may as well move inside." He extinguished it and deposited the butt into a nearby receptacle. "Shall we?"

Sean grabbed the handle of the door. A tremble began beneath him, and he lost his grip. A loud blast, like ten cars backfiring at once, sounded above them. Suddenly, a wave of force pressed at him from above. Glass shards showered down upon the two of them. The sound penetrated his eardrums and a ringing followed.

Coughing and shaking glass from his hair, Sean retreated from the door, following closely behind Woods. They both shook their heads to clear them.

"Oh, my word..." Woods exclaimed, pointing upwards.

Sean craned his neck.

About four stories up the building, a section of the floor had been completely blown away.

7

October 17th
6:30 p.m.

As the smoke curled around them, Sean heard Woods cry out, "Xena! Jean! Franny! They're still in there!" The inspector made a move as if to run back into the building, but Sean grabbed his arm to restrain him.

"You don't know what that bomb did to the structure of the building," Sean told him. His eyes stung from the fumes as he blearily peered upwards once more. Against the mirrored glass of the rest of the building, it looked as if someone had tried to carve a Jack-o-lantern smile. A faint light from still-lit fires danced behind the smoke.

"Those are my *people*," Woods snapped, yanking his arm

away.

Sean took in a deep breath. He knew if it were someone he cared about he'd do the same thing. "Okay. Let's go get them."

Woods paused for less than a breath before giving a curt nod.

The two of them pushed through the glass doors. Suddenly, swarms of people came flooding into the lobby area—most from the staircases, but a few from the elevators—to flee the burning building.

"This way!" Woods shouted to Sean over the rush. They shoved through the masses and found a stairwell, moving against the current to climb up the four flights. Sean coughed and wheezed as the air grew thicker and fuzzier the higher they ascended. Once on the correct floor, Woods flung open the door.

"Wait!" Sean cried out, but he was too late.

Screams punctuated the general shrieks in the stairwell as bystanders got a blast of heat from the burning fire behind the door.

Sean pushed Woods aside and slammed it shut.

"It's no good!" he yelled. "We have to get the rest of these people out of here."

Woods remained still, staring at the recently closed door, his eyes bulging.

"WOODS!" Sean shouted, standing in the British man's way, a breath away from his face. "We have to go, NOW!"

Recognition registered in Woods' eyes and the man gave another tight nod. The two of them corralled the remaining people down the stairs. Sean helped a man who'd been knocked over by the fiery blast and was clutching his ankle. Woods kept everyone moving, sweat pouring down his shaved, dark scalp.

Once outside, Sean could hear the faint sounds of fire trucks making their way towards the disaster. Someone must have called 911 to report the incident. Searching, Sean caught up with Woods.

"You all right?" Sean asked, coughing into the crook of his arm. His lungs hurt when he breathed, and his throat felt scratchy. Tears coursed down his cheeks, working overtime to try to clear the irritants from his eyes.

"I can't..." Woods shook his head, as if trying to calculate multiple things at once. "They're..."

"Woods. Come on, man. Authorities are going to be here any minute. What are we going to tell them?"

A light came into Woods' eyes. "We can't be here." He gripped Sean's arm. "This is an unsanctioned team I put together. No one can know we were here."

Sean let out a sharp breath. "Shit. Right. Of course not. Now we gotta dodge the Boston FD. But what can we do?"

"Bloody hell, I don't know." Woods ran his hand over his head, wiping away several beads of sweat.

Sean did a quick sweep of the area, blinking repeatedly as the wind cleared his eyes. "Where did you park?"

Woods nodded towards the rear of the lot.

"Yeah, I'm there, too," Sean said. "I think we can..." he made a circle motion with his hand.

"I understand."

The fire engine pulled up in front of the building. Sean could hear other sirens close behind.

"We gotta go, now."

The two men eased their way through the crowd, which was thoroughly fixated on the efforts of the fire department. They reached the inspector's car first.

Sean stopped him from getting in. "Where are you heading?"

"To my hotel." Woods' eyes were slightly glazed.

Sean's brow furrowed. "I don't know if that's a good idea. If these arsonists found you here, they may find you where you're staying."

"The...the arsonists?" Recognition flooded Woods' face. "I didn't even think of that! Those bloody bastards!"

"Woods, focus man! I guess...I guess I don't know for sure. I just assumed..."

Woods wiped his sleeve across his brow. Flecks of ash and smears of black darkened his dress shirt. "We both know it has to be them."

Sean peered behind him. Water sprayed from hoses aimed across the front of the building. "We can talk about this once we've gotten out of here."

"I need to go back to my hotel. All my items are in my room. Passport, money, all the data I've collected—"

"None of that will matter if the room is staked out and they find you. Or if it hasn't already been set on fire."

The glazed look cleared, and Woods' eyes widened. "All my research..." He glanced once again at the building. "My team..." His stare hardened.

Sean knew that look all too well. "This isn't the time for revenge. We will figure this out, but right now we gotta leave and you *cannot* go to the hotel." He paused, thinking rapidly. "My place. We can stay there for now." He nodded at his Jag. "Follow my car."

Woods didn't change his eyeline, like a shark locked onto its prey.

"Woods," Sean said, clamping a hand on the man's shoulder. He waited until Woods finally looked at him. "We need to leave."

A third sharp nod. "Very well," he said, his words full of poison. "I will follow you."

8

October 17th
7:00 p.m.

Cold liquid splashed against Charlotte's face. With a sputtering cough, she awoke.

"Wakey, wakey, *Messiah*."

The sharp words reached her through her groggy state and Charlotte did her best to focus. The room came into view slowly. Metallic clanging could be heard to her left, the hissing of steam to her right. Chilly concrete lay underneath her stretched body. She vaguely remembered waking up once, maybe twice, earlier, only to be sedated again.

That cannot be good for me, she thought. Although at this moment, she had no clue as to the time, only that she'd been kidnapped that morning after her jog with Isabella.

Isabella? For a moment, she looked around, expecting to see the Italian woman there to reassure her that everything would be all right. Instead, she remembered her predicament. Isabella was gone. Carla and Jordan had no idea about her location.

She was alone.

Except for the lone figure who sat on a metal folding chair in front of her.

Mags.

Though she probably wasn't Mags. She was the Triad version of Mags. The one who'd murdered her ex-fiancé and Detective Juliette Tay. Even though this woman looked identical, from the cropped brown hair and side-swept bangs to the funky tights and eclectic earrings, the similarities ended there. Lines of hatred etched around her eyes and a sneer on her lips kept her from ever looking like Mags.

Charlotte attempted to reach up and wipe the remaining dripping liquid from her face, but her arm stopped short about halfway through the movement. With a bleary glance, she noted the shackle around her wrist, connected to a steel pipe next to her.

"Where am I?" she asked, the words a touch slurred. She forced herself to sit up, her cold, tight muscles protesting. She must have been laying on the floor for hours. The chill seeped through her to the point at which she felt creaky and stiff. A smidgen of light shone behind her, so she assumed there may be a window, but she didn't dare turn to check. The woman in front of her held her complete attention.

"Funny. You've been so pampered through all this that you actually think I'll tell you."

Another crash of cold liquid.

"Stop!" Charlotte said, spitting out the salty substance. The salinity stung her eyes this time.

The fake Mags spoke again. "You don't have a say in anything. So, you don't *say* anything."

Another wave of water hit her.

Charlotte remained quiet this time.

"Oh good, she understands." The woman leaned forward. "Here's what's going to happen, Princess. You're here until you're not useful anymore. You don't get to know where *here* is. You don't get to know anyone's plan. You don't get to do or say anything unless told to do so." She stood abruptly, knocking the chair backwards. The clang of it hitting the floor echoed in the cement-and-piped-filled room. Charlotte jumped at the noise.

"No more beautiful underground bunkers or nice hotels," she continued, pacing like a caged tiger. "No more campers or safe houses. You've been spoiled because of who everyone thinks you are. But that's not how things fly here."

With a quick movement, the fake Mags crouched down, inches from Charlotte's face. Charlotte did her best not to flinch, but the antipathy pouring from this woman was almost palpable.

"One thing I do want you to know. We own this building. So, you could clang or scream all you want, and it wouldn't make a difference." She roughly wiped some of the liquid from Charlotte's forehead. "But for every noise you *do* make, I'll remove that body part. You want to clang? Say goodbye to your fingers. Scream out? I'll slit your vocal cords."

Charlotte could see the glimmer of greed and wanting in the woman's eyes and her throat went dry. No bluffing here. Even worse, it seemed as if she hoped Charlotte *would* try something for an excuse to do some damage.

The non-Mags pulled away just as quickly. "I'll return with a bottle of water and a bucket for Your Majesty to piss in. Unless sitting in your own slop appeals to you?"

Charlotte, too afraid to say anything, merely shook her head the tiniest bit.

"Smart move." With that, the woman swept out the door, where it slammed closed with a metallic bang. Sounds of a lock clicking into place could be heard shortly after.

Charlotte let out a shuddery breath. Denial no longer remained an option. Mags was indeed a Triad agent, and definitely not afraid to follow through with violence. Her mind wandered, wondering how many times she'd been around this woman instead of Mags and had never known it. Had she inadvertently supplied information to these arsonists without even realizing it?

With a shake of her head, Charlotte pushed away those dark thoughts. There would have been no way she could have known about Mags' relationship with the Triads or the arson group. She couldn't blame herself.

But could she be culpable for her current predicament? If she'd never claimed herself the Messiah, she'd never have been kidnapped.

No, that wasn't true either. Truth had made the Messiah

declaration six months ago. As Isabella had told her, factions had already made attempts on her life.

Isabella, Charlotte thought. A stinging of tears burned behind her eyes, but her lack of hydration kept them from falling. Even though Isabella had been responsible for reviving Charlotte's involvement into all this Triad nonsense, she'd only done so after saving Charlotte's life. She'd offered options, but never pushed. She'd let Charlotte make the decision on her own to claim her Messiah status and promised to do her best to protect Charlotte.

So, who else could help? Only Carla or Jordan. And she and Isabella were supposed to meet Carla right before they'd been taken. Carla would know something went wrong, but what could she do? She wouldn't have any idea who had snatched them from the street, much less her current location.

No one knew where she was. She hadn't left any clues to anyone that she may be in any trouble. Even her voicemail message last night to Sean only suggested she wouldn't be in contact with him for a while. It would be days before he would wonder about her.

A sense of loneliness stole over Charlotte. Up until this point, she hadn't truly been by herself. And even when Truth had abducted her and taken her to the bunker, Charlotte had felt protected.

Now, no one here cared if she got hurt. No one would keep her from being killed.

Think, Charlotte, think. For whatever reason, these arsonists hadn't killed her. At least not yet. Which meant they needed her alive. So, she still held value. At least she had that notion to give her a little comfort.

Charlotte peered around the space once more. She had no doubt of fake Mags' sincerity. She knew any attempt at escape or calling out for help would lead to a severe punishment.

The shackle on her wrist clanged against the pipe connected to it. Aches in her knees and right shoulder throbbed, now that the adrenaline in her system ebbed. Her shoulder blade stung, and she wondered if she'd split the stitches she'd received a week ago. Carla had helped her clean and redress them the previous day and said they'd almost healed, but Charlotte wondered if perhaps the wound had reopened because it prickled like crazy.

Had that only been yesterday? Only one day since she'd claimed herself the Messiah, since the camper had been torched, since she'd been seized by a group of arsonists?

Charlotte didn't give into despair very often, but it currently trembled on the edges of her soul.

A slow drip from a nearby pipe contrasted to a strange scraping sound coming from above her. The thought of where she might be briefly penetrated her hollow thoughts as something to distract her, when the creaking of the door opening drew her attention once more to the entrance of the room.

Fake Mags entered. As promised, a largish bottle of water sat in one hand and the other carried a standard red plastic bucket.

"I hear you've been quiet," the woman said, closing the door behind her. "That's good. Real good."

Charlotte said nothing.

The woman placed the bucket next to Charlotte and the water bottle in front of her. "We'll need to make sure those pretty pipes are kept moist."

The questioning word, "Why?", almost spilled from her lips, but she caught herself.

Fake Mags grinned. Charlotte was forcibly reminded of the Cheshire Cat from *Alice in Wonderland*. "They told me you were quick. I kinda hoped you wouldn't be."

Charlotte gestured towards the bottle.

"Help yourself. And use the bucket when you need to."

Charlotte twisted off the cap and took a slug, the room temperature water swilling around in her dry mouth. Once the dryness had been sated a bit, she drank down half the bottle. The liquid sloshed in her empty belly.

"I'm sure you're wondering what we have planned for you. You must have noticed you're not dead."

Charlotte nodded. She noticed the use of the word "we," signifying this woman was not working alone. And possibly, not giving orders, but instead the one receiving them.

Fake Mags stared down at her. "Well, I'm not some monologuing villain from a Bond movie. You'll know things as I tell you. In the meantime, be happy we want you alive. Enjoy your stay here. I'll return in the morning."

Charlotte could feel all the words and questions she wanted to say pressing against the inside of her lips, but she kept her mouth clamped shut. Her gaze followed the fake Mags out of the room, and she let out a shuddering breath when the door slammed shut.

9

October 17th
7:30 p.m.

Sean snatched up some dirty clothes from the couch and tossed them towards the open closet, in which his laundry basket sat. Most of them made it inside, but he figured Woods wouldn't care too much, especially because he still seemed in shock. Not that Sean could blame him. He'd just lost his whole team in a moment's time.

"Make yourself at home," Sean said, gesturing to the couch.

Woods sank down onto the cushy seating, his eyes a bit distant once more.

"Beer?" Sean asked, not really sure what else to do.

"No thanks. I don't drink. Gave it up with smoking. Although that's not been going the best." He let out a curt laugh. "Ironically enough, having that cigarette tonight probably saved my life." A dark look crossed his face.

Sean grabbed a beer for himself from the fridge and sat next to the Interpol agent. He took a swig. "Sorry about your team," he said. Normally the words were just to fill space—he'd told them many times to people who'd lost someone—but this time they held weight. The names of those he'd lost crawled through his own head, from Angellica to Tay to Mags...even Charlotte could be considered a loss. They weren't all dead, but they were all lost. "Maybe they got out okay? We saw a lot of people running from the building. Maybe the explosion's epicenter was closer to the windows or one of them was in the bathroom?"

"I hate that I can't go there and find out," Woods said, his voice low almost a growl.

"I know, but I'll try to find out what I can from the fire department in the morning, if I can without arousing any suspicion."

Woods ran a hand over his shorn scalp, his fingers shaking. "After the deaths of Simone and Tam, I promised the others I'd be more careful, that we'd all be safe."

Sean remembered that Woods told him his group had lost others during their work on the Triads. "Those are...other agents?"

"Tam, yes, out of Hong Kong. Simone was not an agent. She worked as a Historian in Lyon. Her focus was Meso-potamia and the Sumerian culture. She'd apparently discovered a possible connection to an earlier civilization. Inspector De'leu worked the most with her. They grew...close."

"An earlier civilization..." Sean muttered out loud. "This Simone woman, she somehow found out about that Book. The one we found in the underground bunker, which was stolen on the day of Violet's trial."

"In a way, yes, though she didn't know the full extent of her discovery at the time. It wasn't until the Book's existence was revealed during the hearing that my team fully understood what Simone had stumbled across. But by that time, Simone had already been killed—hit and run."

Sean took another slug of beer. He had no doubt in his mind that Simone's "car crash" had been orchestrated by a Triad agent. The number of "accidents" under the guise of them covering their tracks were just too many to ignore as coincidence. "How did she learn about the Book stuff?"

"A packet had been mailed to her with several pages included—all of which were written in the pre-Sumerian text."

"Who sent the packet?"

"Anonymous mailer."

Sean rolled the beer bottle between his hands, thinking. He now knew the Triads existed, but he'd forgotten not only their expansion across the world, but also how long they'd been in existence. "Can I ask what happened with Agent Tam?"

Woods let out a long sigh and Sean wondered if he'd pushed too hard. But Sean knew they didn't have much time to waste. These Triads had no problem continuing to kill. And people Sean knew were involved as well—Mags working with them, Charlotte dealing with them, Tay dying from them...

And Inspector Woods wasn't out of the line of danger either. Someone would discover he hadn't died in that explosion and would come searching for him. It wouldn't take long for him to become connected to Sean, either. Woods had been to the precinct twice—the first time asking about Tay, the second time for Sean. And if the Triad agent who'd set off the explosion in the building had remained nearby, they may have seen Sean with Woods in the parking lot.

Either way, Sean found himself on borrowed time as well.

Finally, Woods replied, idly rubbing his fingers across the sofa's fabric. "Tam was a retired police officer out of Hong Kong. Mid-sixties or so. In his final years, he'd been appointed to look through cold cases. One of these cases involved a woman who'd been found standing amongst three other women—all dead. She'd been covered with their blood, a knife in her hand. When arrested, this woman, Yao Qi, babbled on about no longer wanting to be 'the savior.' Though Tam always said the translation was more akin to 'Messiah' than 'savior.'"

A bolt of electric adrenaline shot through Sean. "Messiah?" he said, the word catching in his throat. An image of Charlotte's face popped into his head, and he could hear her words on the clip Elaine had played for him repeating in his mind. *"I am the Messiah."*

Woods scratched his head, as if his responses were automatic, but his mind was calculating something else at the same time. "Yes. He'd been insistent that the case held more significance but refused to disclose anything to me until we met in person. Up until then, we'd only corresponded long-distance."

"Let me guess. Some mishap occurred before you could

meet up with him?"

Woods gave a curt nod, his hands moving to his lap where they twisted together. "Heart attack. Before the plane even landed." Suddenly, he sprang from the couch. "How could the arsonists have found us?" he said, abruptly changing topics. "It doesn't make any bloody sense. We were so careful. I screened everyone. Checked backgrounds. We weren't even officially sanctioned by Interpol, so they would not be able to acknowledge our work or disclose our location to anyone. Not that they could. Even *they* didn't know where we'd set up base." Woods paced next to the arm of the couch. "No one knew except Detective Tay and yourself." He paused, facing Sean.

Sean held his hands up, defensive. "I didn't tell anyone, I swear. And Tay never told me. I didn't even know she was meeting your team until you showed up at the precinct."

"Perhaps she told someone else? A spouse?"

Sean shook his head. "She wasn't married. And she's not the gossiping type. Wasn't," he corrected himself, cringing at the now past tense.

"Well, someone knew we'd be in that building."

Sean ran his fingers through his hair. His head spun with thoughts. There were too many loose ends, too many paths. He needed to get ahead of these women, stop playing catch-up. This whole situation needed to be narrowed down.

Only one person he knew had any other information.

"I need to make a quick phone call. The reception in here sucks so..." he said, pointing at his front door. "Feel free to watch TV. We can order some takeout when I'm done."

"Of course." Woods straightened his shoulders. "I appreciate your help, Detective Trann."

"You can drop the 'detective.' And not a problem." Sean paused before stepping outside the apartment. "You can't check on them, you know."

A droop in the inspector's shoulders. "I know. Every molecule in me wants to call my team members' hotels and see if they've returned or check with hospitals, but…" He clasped his hands in front of him. "I know if I do and they are alive, I could expose them, or myself. I'll wait."

Sean's gaze softened because he knew how much trouble he'd have keeping quiet if the situation were reversed. "Be right back." He walked down the hall where there was better reception and called Elaine. She answered on the third ring.

"Hey Sean!" she answered. "I was just thinking of calling you. I've got some news."

His stomach tightened. What could she possibly reveal now? How much more damage could he handle?

"Before you say anything," he cut in, "I have to ask you something."

A pause. Sean could almost *hear* the irritation in it. "All right. What?

"Some new developments have come up on my end as well. As a result, I want to combine the people working on this whole 'arson-Triad' thing together."

Another pause. "What *kind* of people?"

Sean hesitated. Both sides didn't want their identities revealed. But if he wanted them to join forces…

"Someone I know has also been working on this case. I will ask them if they're comfortable working with you, too, before I reveal either of you to each other."

"Are they trustworthy?"

Sean thought about everything Woods had accomplished and sacrificed. "Yeah."

"And you think they could really help?"

"I think each of you has information that, alone, isn't enough. It's time to team up."

Several beats passed. "I don't know if bringing in someone new is a good idea..."

"They aren't new. They've actually been at it longer than we have. I only just found out recently."

"Hm...well, if you think it'll be okay, then I suppose I'm game."

A breath of relief exited his lungs. "Great. Let me check on this end. If it works out, could you stop by my apartment sometime this week? The sooner, the better."

"I could come tomorrow evening."

"That'll work. But let me check with my other person. I'll call you again in a few."

"Wait, I have news, too!"

Sean waited.

"There was an explosion like an hour ago at an office building. I'm covering the story, but they suspect arson. Could be one of ours?"

Sean's heart raced. "Listen, be careful. You may be more right than you know." He wondered if she could get news faster than he about Woods' team." Learn everything you can—especially about survivors—but don't poke too hard. I'll call soon."

"Okay, but—"

Sean hung up and went inside his apartment. He knew she probably wanted to talk more, but he had to keep focused. One step at a time.

Woods had turned on some black-and-white movie with subtitles, though his upright posture made Sean think the man was simply staring at the screen and not really watching the film.

"Hey, man," Sean said.

Woods glanced up.

Sean said, "So...there's something I'd like to ask you about. And I realize the timing might not be the best, but I don't know if we have any other choice."

"What is it?"

"I'd like to bring someone else in to go over all this arson/Triad stuff."

Silence.

Sean's brow furrowed. "I know this is a lot to ask, especially because of what happened tonight. Normally I wouldn't, tell you there's time, but I don't know how much time is left. These Triad women are strategically finding people who know about them and removing them. I'm sure they know about you. If we don't do everything we can to expose them as quickly as possible, I wouldn't be surprised if they figure out a way to find you. Eventually."

The words hung in the air. Sean was banking on the hope that this man would somehow keep his professionalism during this horrible situation. If the tables were turned...

They have *been turned,* Sean thought to himself as a

reminder. *And you almost gave up.* But he had someone to revive his interest.

Charlotte.

Sean swallowed against the lump in his throat. He couldn't think about her, not right now, or *he* wouldn't stay professional either.

"I can't tell you what to do," Sean continued slowly. "All I know is that I'm tired of losing people I care about. I'm sick of losing team members. And it seems like at this point, if these Triads don't already know I'm investigating, they will soon enough. I don't think I can cover my tracks anymore. And you've been really good at it so far, but now they caught up to you, too."

Woods looked away, staring blankly at the television.

"This person I know, they've been investigating into the situation as well. They are smart and have some good leads. But they're stuck. I can figure this whole mess out, I know I can, but something is missing. I don't think we can do it without what you both know to tie everything together."

Sean waited, watching the man in front of him, wondering if he could hold things together or if he would break.

A steely resolute look crossed over Woods' dark eyes, and he returned his gaze to Sean. "I want this finished. I want them caught. Whatever needs to be done, I'll oblige."

Relief slid over Sean. "Great. She'll be able to come over tomorrow night. I just have to give her a call and confirm. And..." he continued, "she may have updates on your team."

Woods gave a knowing look. "Reporter?"

Sean nodded.

"They do tend to engrain themselves into the Triad world," Woods added.

"I suppose it's their job to investigate and as good as these women are, everyone makes mistakes at some point."

"Agreed. Though eventually they dig too deep and become targets themselves." His shoulders straightened. "What do you suggest is our next step?"

"Let me call Elaine, first, and let her know the plan. Then we'll strategize." Sean stepped out into the hallway and placed the call.

"Hey Elaine," he said, after she answered.

"Well?"

Sean could hear the curtness in her tone and knew she must be upset that he cut her off earlier. "He's agreed to work with you, with us. You still able to come tomorrow night?"

"Yes, I can swing by around seven-ish."

"Perfect." He cleared his throat. "So, what was your news?"

A quiet huff, but when she began talking, no lingering traces of resentment remained. "Remember that audio clip we heard?"

Sean's hand tightened on the phone. Had Elaine discovered it was Charlotte's voice?

"Yeah..."

"Well, I've been monitoring the site and they posted something new. Another partial clip. Sounded like the same woman."

A lump the size of a baseball sat in his throat. "What did it say?"

"Two short bursts of words. First one was..." flipping of

pages. "'Alert all agents.' And the second one was 'I will provide a new direction for the Triads.' So, it definitely sounds like whatever the outcome is includes all the Triad members. I mean, this is a huge break. The guy who runs the site must have a direct line to whoever sent out this message. He said on his website he will reveal more snippets as he receives them, which means someone is supplying him with these messages. It may just be to drive up views, but either way, we gotta talk to him."

"All right. I'll figure out a way to track this guy down. In the meantime, keep monitoring that website. And...there was another one too, right?"

"Yeah, but I haven't really checked that one in a while. It's been pretty dormant."

"Still...that one had agent names listed. None of the other websites had that." His mind started to swirl. "I bet whoever runs that website has more of a link than this audio clip guy."

"No way. He's playing actual proof."

"But he's being fed the information, which means he doesn't control what he receives. Someone posting actual agent names sounds like their connection is more concrete. *And* you said the site existed and posted stuff before the Triad trial even started. That means it had previous knowledge before any Triad stuff had been made public."

A pause. "I guess so."

Sean shook his head, a yawn escaping his mouth. "Listen, keep following both websites, just in case. And send me the links. I'll track down their owners tomorrow so we can follow up with them. Then, when we meet tomorrow night, we'll put everything together."

"I'll put an alert on my phone to let me know any time something new is posted. See you tomorrow."

"Night, Elaine."

Sean hung up and reentered his apartment. He was about to tell Woods about the conversation, but instead the sight of the British man fast asleep, his head to one side, greeted him. He thought about waking him but figured any sleep would be elusive enough. Woods should probably get it while he could.

Speaking of, Sean yawned again. He should follow his own advice.

10

October 17th
9:00 p.m.

Jordan Parker, District Attorney, could not stop tapping her finger on the arm of the chair.

She hadn't heard anything from Carla since that morning when she'd been told to stay put in her apartment.

"Isabella and Charlotte did not show up at our meeting place," Carla had said, her Spanish lilt stronger than usual.

"What can I do?" Jordan had asked.

"Nothing. Just stay where you are. I will call you if I find them or, if I don't, I will contact you tomorrow. Do not speak with anyone else. Call in sick to work today and tomorrow. Do not leave your place."

That had been over 12 hours ago, and Jordan had been going stir crazy. She reorganized her bookshelves, cleaned each room from top to bottom, watched a slew of science fiction movies, and nibbled on anything she had remaining in the place, since she'd planned to go grocery shopping after work today.

The sun had set, the room darkened, and still, no call.

Jordan had gotten used to the waiting over the past couple of years, since she'd first joined up with Isabella and Carla's cause. Isabella represented the brains, Carla the brawn. Jordan...well it took a while for her to find her niche, but she had a lot of excellent skills that came in handy. Reading people, gathering resources, searching through criminal files to find other possible Triad members.

But the one area she lacked? Self-defense.

She'd begged each woman independently to teach her and they'd both refused. They said they didn't want her to go down their own path.

"You aren't a killer," Isabella had said. "Don't be so eager to change into one."

"If one of these women comes after me, I should be able to protect myself."

"We'll make sure you're safe."

Carla had a different approach. "You would lose."

Jordan had scoffed. "Not if you teach me."

With a pitying facial expression, Carla continued. "I don't say this to offend you, I say it because against any Triad woman, you would fail. It isn't just learning to defend yourself, it's about being more cutthroat, more devious, and more willing to not only defend yourself, but to end them. You aren't cut out for that."

"How do you know unless you give me a chance?"

Carla's expression hardened. "Because I did my research. Reality is, you shouldn't even be a part of all this, but you stumbled onto the Triads and your position within the law has been useful. The other alternative was to kill you, but I don't want to kill innocents anymore."

The words had stung, but Jordan came to see the wisdom in them. Carla had been right. At the time, becoming a fighter hadn't been the role for her.

When Jordan first joined up, the whole idea of hunting down Triads and stopping them from hurting and slaughtering innocents had seemed noble. Vigilantes bent on stopping those the law could not. But after a while, the process felt a bit... pointless.

Yes, they'd stopped several Triad groups and even more thirds, but the numbers weren't making much of a difference.

Jordan had tried to pitch ways to help speed the process along—mostly through exposure. She understood how the Triads did everything possible to *stop* exposure, but whenever she brought up the subject, Isabella and Carla cringed, vetoing the idea almost immediately. At first, Jordan thought their blockage had to do with strategy, but the more she learned about these women and the Triads, the more she believed Isabella and Carla were acting out of habit instead. They were *used* to not wanting to expose the Triads because that's what they'd been taught by the very same institution they now sought to destroy.

So, Jordan started to take matters into her own hands. She felt no need to share her idea with the other two. They had their hands full already. Instead, she implemented her own strategy with the ultimate goal of exposure: she contacted a website and began feeding the owner information about the Triads.

Her most recent and largest contribution had been providing the website with audio clips of Charlotte's message claiming herself as the Messiah. She hoped to draw out Triad members who would target the website owner to shut him down. Security measures had been put into place—with the owner, Zack's, blessing—to alert her of any trouble. He was charged with spacing out these clips to draw more attention.

But after this morning's abduction of Charlotte and Isabella, Jordan grew worried that she wouldn't be able to provide clips anymore, especially if they needed to go on the run again. The chance to send snippets would be stamped out if Carla stood hovering over Jordan's shoulder.

Instead, Jordan gave Zack access to a Triad email account, provided to him from the return pings on some of the accounts which opened after the original Charlotte speech. Jordan told him to monitor that email—which was set for "receive only"— and to continue posting any audio clips as he obtained them.

Satisfied that she'd contributed in some way, Jordan then went about her day keeping herself as distracted as possible. But as the hours whittled away and Carla didn't call, Jordan's nerves escalated. Just in case, she packed two "to go" bags, so she could leave on a moment's notice. And she started to have second thoughts about deceiving the other women.

"I'll tell them next time I see them," she promised.

Finally, at about 9 p.m. that night, a knock sounded on her door.

"Oh, thank goodness," she exclaimed. Briskly strolling towards the door, she paused a foot away from it.

"Who is it?"

Silence.

Jordan placed an eye up to the peephole.

The door suddenly smashed inward, breaking at the deadbolt, and bashing her head-on.

Jordan stumbled backwards. White spots floated around her. Pain flared across her nose. Placing her hands on her face, they came away bloody.

Two people entered. One, a man she'd never seen before. The other, Mags.

No, Jordan thought, fear escalating to horror inside her. *Not Mags. A Triad third.*

"Knock knock," fake Mags said. "Can we come in?"

"What do you want?" Jordan sputtered, spraying a few specks of blood as she spoke.

"Boss wants you dead," the man said, glancing around her apartment.

Her eyes widened, then she frantically peered around the area, searching for any kind of weapons, whatever she could use to defend herself.

But nothing in her cozy living room provided any help. She was a mouse, caught in the corner by two hungry cats.

"Boss is disappointed in you," fake Mags went on, pulling a knife from her jacket pocket.

"Why? I don't even know your boss." Jordan didn't know

what she was saying. Words simply came out as her anxiety reached new heights.

Fake Mags simply smiled, a toothy grin that stretched nearly from ear to ear.

"Get what we need," she said to the man. "I'll take care of her."

"You always get to have the fun," the man said, winking.

"I had a long day. Took ages to get the smoke smell out of my hair. I need something...easy."

The man shrugged, as if doing nothing more than giving up his seat in a car instead of relinquishing the chance to murder someone.

Fake Mags approached her, slinking through the space between them.

"Too bad it'll be done so quick," she murmured.

The last thought Jordan recalled before three slices of searing pain caused oblivion to overtake her was the notion that she'd made a difference in the world.

And if she had the chance, she'd do it again.

Because one day, women like fake Mags would no longer exist.

11

October 18th
5:30 a.m.

Mae felt a grin spread across her face after she took one last glance at their prisoner before closing the heavy door behind her. She nodded at the guard stationed outside the door. It felt so good to be restored in her own body—once again able to help the Triads steer themselves onto the right path. And now she didn't have to deal with switching back and forth into her obnoxiously lovable spinoff personality, Mags.

That's because this time things would be different. No more fake personas. No more restrictions on hunting. United, the Triads would rise to a time of glory, where their true purpose would be carried out under one leadership.

With a whistle on her lips, Mae made her way down the corridor of the warehouse.

She had a quick, easy assignment she still looked forward to after such a long day and then just a short speech to prepare for little miss "Messiah..."

Mags fought to stay conscious. She didn't want to prepare a speech. She didn't want to keep someone locked up, under guard. She didn't want the Triads to win!

With a gasp, she awoke. It took her several seconds to take in her surroundings, which were completely unfamiliar. Once again, no light seeped in around the curtains from outside, but this time the lamp on the side table had been left on. Gray wallpaper with little flecks of silver greeted her under the bluish tint of the lampshade.

A hotel room. A different one, from the looks of it. Because I'm Mae.

Tremors shook her at the thought.

No time for this. Deep breath. Relax.

First bit of good news—she was alone in the bed this time.

Second was that she had a plan.

Flinging away the puffy cream comforter, Mags stepped out of bed, the air cool on her nearly naked body. She dressed swiftly, ignoring the call of her bladder, and made her way to the Business Center of the hotel. Logging in, she quickly bypassed security protocols on the Boston police department precinct computers and sent an encrypted email to Sean.

Gathering her thoughts, she pulled on all she could remember from her past dreams, or in actuality, her memories as Mae.

Unaware of how much time she might have before she reverted to Mae's consciousness, she typed as fast as she could, not bothering to doublecheck for errors or repetition.

Sean,

This may come as a shock to you, but if anyone will believe me, it's you, cuz of Angellica. I'm Mags, but I'm actually a Triad agent, a woman named Mae. I have moments of clarity, it seems, around 5 or 6 in the morning. Not sure why, maybe due to her sleep cycle or Ceridian timings. Either way, I needed to send you something to let you know what's going on.

I've been having dreams—more like flashes—of what Mae has been doing. Yesterday morning after I woke, I saw that she received a message for a new target. That means she's in direct contact with whoever is orchestrating these fires. The group planned a meeting last night at around 8pm. I don't know what happened during it, but it sounded like the timetable of revealing themselves or their motives has been pushed up. Because I, well she, got put on the news for Juliette's...

Mags' fingers trembled. She couldn't bring herself to finish the sentence.

Twenty minutes had already come and gone. Mags felt the first inkling of pain between her eyebrows.

I'm almost out of time, she thought.

Her fingers flying, she continued to type.

This a.m. I saw M in some sort of warehouse. Sean—she

has Char locked up, under guard. She's excited about the Triads moving forward. I don't know what the plan is for Char...

A pang of pain.

"No, no, no," she muttered, her hand pressing against her skull.

Too late. She couldn't risk being out of bed and alerting Mae that she still existed. But she needed just a few more words.

I can't let you find me yet. C is at risk. I don't even know if I can write to you again. I may never come back.

PANG!

Her sight blurring, Mags finished with one last sentence before hitting *Send* and racing away back to the hotel room.

If I do, I'll email you tomorrow a.m.

12

October 18th
7:00 a.m.

"Wakey, wakey."

Briny water once again hit Charlotte in the face. She sputtered, her eyes adjusting to both the lights and the liquid in them. Once able to, she concentrated on her abductor—fake Mags.

A new bottle of water moved in front of her. Charlotte reached up and took it, cracked it open, and chugged a third of the bottle in one go.

"Thirsty this morning, I see," the alternate version of Mags said.

You have given me one bottle of water since I got here,

Charlotte retorted in her head. Based on the angle of sunlight creeping through the window behind her, she guessed the sun had recently risen. That put her at being held for about twenty-four hours with no food, one bottle of water, and a freezing cold floor on which she'd fitfully dozed all night. Her whole body felt achy and heavy, and she knew that if this kept up for too long, she'd get sick.

Or die.

Fake Mags sat cross-legged in front of her, a sneer on her face.

It was so strange to see such a look on the woman Charlotte had spent three months with traipsing around the world, looking for proof of Triads. It felt like a different lifetime, even though they'd only returned about four weeks ago.

How could Charlotte not have seen the signs? How could she have spent so much time with Mags and not noticed any inconsistencies? Sure, they spent plenty of time apart, but if Mags had been switched to this fake version, wouldn't Charlotte have noticed?

Except Isabella said after Truth exposed her Triad that many "sleeper" agents were kept in their docile states. Perhaps Mags was merely Mags that whole time. There would have been nothing for me to uncover.

Yet there was no mistaking the difference now. This woman in front of her may look like Mags, but she carried no other stylistic traits. Even the slight shift in the way she dressed—still argyle and plaid, but more blacks and grays, tighter clothes. Her hair was flatter and less funky. Even the way she sat—cocky and...perched to pounce. Like she couldn't wait for Charlotte to make a mistake so she could swoop in and catch her.

Charlotte took another smaller sip, determined to save the rest for the remainder of the day. She wasn't sure if she'd be given anything more to drink, much less to eat. Charlotte had done her best to ignore her growling stomach, but the cold concrete beneath her and the digging of the shackle on her wrist offered little distraction.

Fake Mags said nothing, just grinning her Cheshire cat grin.

Charlotte did not take the bait. She sat, returning the stare.

Finally, fake Mags spoke. "How'd you sleep?"

A direct question. According to what fake Mags said yesterday, she could respond if asked or told something directly.

"Not well," Charlotte replied, her voice cracking from lack of use.

"Oooh, not sounding too hot. I'll fix that, don't worry."

A shot of anxiety flushed through Charlotte's system. She didn't know what "fixing" entailed so she was definitely felt concerned.

"I'm impressed by you, though disappointed in the situation. I'd hoped you would have tried to escape or something."

Charlotte wanted to reply, but once again, kept her mouth shut.

Fake Mags gave a snort. "This is no fun. You're too smart. I like the dumber ones."

I bet you do, Charlotte thought. If nothing else, this

woman would be as intelligent as Mags was. Which means she may believe herself to be above those with lesser intelligence. It probably gave her a sense of satisfaction to trick others. Charlotte would have to remain on guard.

"Anyhoo, I won't keep you long. Got something I want you to do. Need to make sure you're ready."

Charlotte remained quiet.

"Do you have any allergies?"

Charlotte blinked a few times, caught off guard by the abrupt change in conversation. "Not that I am aware of." She liked that her voice sounded a little steadier.

"Good to know."

Those three words, though seemingly innocuous, made Charlotte's skin tighten. She almost wondered if this woman *wanted* her to be allergic to something but was supposed to make sure she wasn't. Again, this positively led to the idea that someone else was guiding fake Mags along her current path.

"How's your bucket working out?"

"It serves its purpose." Charlotte internally cringed at how awkward it had been to squat above the round plastic bucket to relieve herself. At one point it nearly tipped over and she'd imagined laying in a puddle, since she couldn't mop it up or move somewhere else in the room, like a caged animal with no trainer to clean the area.

"Anything more you need?"

The question hung in the air like a steel trap waiting to catch its prey. The words once again held the tinge of reluctance, as if Mae had been made to ask instead of wanting to ask.

Charlotte hesitated for a moment. How should she

answer? Truthfully? Pridefully? Stubbornly? She was forcibly reminded of her kidnapping from Truth six months ago. Charlotte had been leery then as well, though much more comfortable physically. She'd debated at that time how to answer Truth's questions, too.

It all depends on the person asking the question.

Truth had wanted Charlotte to be as relaxed as possible, holding her in a state of reverence. This woman, here, now? Not as much.

Finally, Charlotte replied in the only way she knew how to get more information about the duration of her stay and the conditions during that time.

"I could use some warmer items—a jacket, blanket, pillow, and gloves. And something to eat." If they wanted her dead would have no need to keep her from getting sick or starving to death. But if they planned to keep her here for a while, and healthy, they'd give her the items.

Fake Mags tilted her head to one side. "I'll find out if anyone wants to bother. See you in a bit."

As soon as fake Mags closed the door, Charlotte let out a sigh of relief. Now she knew for sure—this woman took orders from someone else. Not only that, but she also had to check before she did anything. And finally, this woman didn't know the whole plan. If she did, she would have already had an answer to Charlotte's request.

Knowing all this didn't help her get any closer to freedom, but at least it meant someone had a plan for her. And a plan meant they wouldn't want her dead.

Yet.

13

October 18th
8:30 a.m.

A restless night of dreams, dotted with floating "Charlotte-heads," and running from explosions kept Sean from feeling any sense of being awake that morning. At the station he found himself in equal-looking company as both Wilt and Millan appeared bleary-eyed and yawning as well. The whole precinct, in fact, seemed unusually subdued. Sean supposed the initial shock of Mags having killed Detective Tay had worn off a bit in the past three days and now the methodical grind of dealing with the aftermath had taken over.

Three days. Had it only been a few days ago?

The entire police force itself had made no progress finding

Mags. Only the tip line provided any leads and those hadn't gone anywhere.

Not that it surprised Sean. Now that he knew about Mags' involvement with the Triads and arsonists, he understood why no one could find her. Those women were thorough in their ability to cover their tracks. Because of this, Sean felt very little motivation to follow normal procedures. All he wanted to do was use police resources to find the owners of those two websites—the one which listed agent names and the one which posted the audio clip of Charlotte. He had a gut feeling that one of them would be able to provide information to move forward in the investigation.

"Hey, Trann," Wilt said as Sean walked by. "You think I could get a ride with you on Monday? My car's making a weird grinding noise so I'm taking it to the shop after work tonight. I doubt it'll be ready until after the weekend and this place doesn't do rentals."

Sean struggled to find the meaning behind Wilt's words. "Monday? What's Monday?"

"Juliette's funeral. Didn't you get the email yesterday afternoon?"

A stone sank into his stomach. The funeral. He'd completely forgotten that there would be a funeral. It was a perfectly normal thing to do when someone died, and yet the thought never crossed his mind.

Sean shook his head. "Haven't checked my emails since yesterday morning."

A look of trepidation crossed Wilt's face. "Well, you are going to be able to go, right?"

Sean nodded. "Of course, man. And don't worry. I'll give you a ride."

Wilt's shoulders relaxed. "Good. Millan said he's going to leave a skeleton crew at the precinct for the afternoon of the funeral. That way most of us can go."

"That's a good idea." Sean cleared his throat as he headed towards his office. A bevy of emotions got caught in his chest. He'd barely even thought of Tay since her murder. All his attention had been on Mags as the killer. Something inside him must have simply clicked off, allowing him to continue working without having to feel any grief. Now, as his computer hummed to life, part of him wanted to skip reading any emails to avoid the one that would confirm in black and white that Tay would never be returning.

His hand hovered over the mouse.

Get it over with, he thought.

With more force than was probably necessary, Sean clicked to open his email account. There, fifth email down, was the email entitled: *Funeral Details for our beloved Juliette Tay.* About to open it, a different email at the top of the list caught his eye. Sent that morning at 6:04 a.m. entitled: *I wish I could make you my special coffee...*

All the breath constricted in his lungs. Those words. There is only one person who would have sent him an email with that subject line.

Mags.

Sean's eyes darted around in their sockets, checking that no one was near. Part of him knew he should let his sergeant know he'd received a possible email from their top priority target, but the other part, the one that knew about Triads, gave a much stronger case for staying quiet.

See what it says first. Then, if it's safe, you can show Millan and Wilt.

Safe. Sean knew he was lying to himself. He wanted to make sure it didn't reveal anything about Charlotte.

Either way, he couldn't make a decision until he opened the email. He leaned closer, drinking in each word. Towards the end, he noticed how she abbreviated more, as if rushed for time.

Sean,

This may come as a shock to you, but if anyone will believe me, it's you, because of Angellica. I'm Mags, but I'm actually a Triad agent, a woman named Mae. I have moments of clarity, it seems, around 5 or 6 in the morning. Not sure why, maybe due to her sleep cycle or Ceridian timings. Either way, I needed to send you something to let you know what's going on.

I've been having dreams—more like flashes—of what Mae has been doing. Yesterday morning, I saw that she received a message for a new target. That means she's in direct contact with whoever is orchestrating these fires. The group planned a meeting last night at around 8pm. I don't know what happened during it, but it sounded like the timetable of revealing themselves or their motives has been pushed up. Because I, well she, got put on the news for Juliette's...

This a.m. I saw M in some sort of warehouse. Sean—she has Char locked up, under guard. She's excited about the Triads moving forward. I don't know what the plan is for Char...

I can't let you find me yet. C is at risk. I don't even know if I can write to you again. I may never come back.

If I do come back, I'll email you tomorrow a.m.

The words penetrated his core, causing him to sink further into his chair. Here it was, confirmation that Mags was indeed a Triad agent. Except, she was claiming that she wasn't.

Just like his ex-fiancée, Angellica.

Sean had worked on the idea in therapy that Angellica could have been two people, but he'd never truly admitted it to himself. And yet, he'd seen it with his own eyes. It wasn't acting. It wasn't pretend. She'd really been split into two different people.

He'd wanted to consider it like a split personality, and in a lot of ways, it was. Except the docile personality was created, not the other way around. These women were murderers in real life and someone else covered that up with a non-psychotic person.

Like Mags.

The woman who'd brought him her special blend of coffee when he'd had a rough day. The friend who'd convinced him to go for a relationship with Charlotte.

Was this really a different person than the one who'd killed Juliette in cold blood?

Before he could think much more about what Mags had written about herself and her alter-ego, the section about Charlotte being held hostage dug in.

Even though she was in a dire situation, a rush of relief

washed over Sean. She was alive. Maybe not perfectly safe, but at least alive. And he *knew* Charlotte couldn't have left that message about being the Messiah of her own accord. She'd been coerced. She had to have been.

And yet...something nagged at the back of Sean's mind. Charlotte's voicemail. She'd mentioned she'd been working on a case—a case she felt would benefit from her involvement. She'd also said she thought she was doing the right thing, that she would contribute to making the world a better place.

That voicemail sounded like she'd *chosen* to help the Triads.

Mags' email about Charlotte being a prisoner didn't quite match up with that idea.

Except...if there was more than one Triad...maybe...

One thing at a time, he reasoned, refocusing his thoughts. He reread the email, taking in the important points.

1) Mags was a Triad agent.
2) She claimed her alternate persona, named Mae, was part of the arson group.
3) The arson group planned to announce their motives, though what the declaration pertained to and who it would be directed at remained unclear.
4) Mae had locked up Charlotte in a warehouse—plan unknown, whereabouts unknown.
5) Mags would try to contact Sean again in the morning, *if* she could.

That "if" hung in the air. If Mags was the fake persona, she could disappear at any moment. She was taking a huge risk sending him this message. If Mae found out Mags was returning to her docile personality, he was sure her Triad group would erase her permanently.

Just like Mags to do something crazy like this... A touch of a smile reached his mouth at the thought of her. He couldn't imagine how terrifying it must have been to realize she was an agent. Not only that, but a made-up person as well.

In this moment, thinking these thoughts, Sean realized he'd accepted the reality of the Triads, of fake personas, and of Mags being innocent. The notions scared him. He preferred living in the world of concrete proof, of tangibility. But the world of the Triads? They followed their own rules the rest of the world didn't know about.

Sean ran his fingers through his hair as he thought about his options. Here, in black and white, was proof of Mags. In the eyes of the law, she was even sort of, kind of, confessing to having killed Juliette. And, in a way, claiming she'd kidnapped Charlotte. If he submitted this email to Millan or told Wilt, they'd pursue her for these reasons. If caught, they'd find out about Charlotte's involvement as well. Even worse, other Triad agents would do what they had to cover their tracks. Mags would probably end up dead, they'd kill Charlotte, and then move their little arson plan somewhere else.

Resolve hit him. He couldn't submit this email as evidence. The world he worked in wouldn't understand. And even if it did, anyone involved would just become targets for the Triads to remove, to minimize exposure.

"Trann?"

Wilt's voice made him jump.

"Yeah, man, what's up?" he said, tilting his monitor from Wilt's view.

"Millan wants us in his office again."

"Of course. Yeah, I'll be right there."

Once Wilt walked away, Sean returned his gaze to his computer. He wasn't sure what to do with the email. He feared leaving it on his work computer, in case someone found it. Should he forward it to his personal email? Print out a paper copy for future reference? Or delete it, just in case?

Before he could decide, a message popped up on his screen: MESSAGE TIMED OUT.

Sean clicked on the "Okay" box beneath the message and the email self-deleted.

Mags, Sean thought. Leave it to her to create an email that would "self-destruct" after a certain amount of time.

He missed her.

Turning off his computer, he thought, *God, I hope I'm doing the right thing...*

14

October 18th
2:00 p.m.

Charlotte wasn't sure which made more noise—her rumbling belly or her chattering teeth.

Fake Mags hadn't bothered to return. Though Charlotte wasn't sure about the exact time of day, she did note the shift of sunlight, which no longer shone directly through the window, indicating several hours must have passed.

Her whole body ached from shivering. Maybe the "powers-that-be" didn't care about keeping her around after all. Constant hissing and dripping from the surrounding pipes became white noise in the background. Her head repeatedly dropped and jerked as she fell in and out of a sporadic doze.

Squealing metal from the door opening reached her through the haze.

Fake Mags entered, a bundle in one hand, a plastic bag hanging from the other.

Though she despised this woman, Charlotte couldn't help but feel a sense of relief at her approach, and what she hoped were provisions. Her stomach lurched at the hope of food, her body spasming at the idea of warmth.

Sure enough, fake Mags dropped the bundle down first, displaying items meant to warm her. Its contents spilled over, showing a pair of sweatpants and socks, two thin blankets, and a square throw pillow. None of the items matched, though they at least looked intact.

"Here," fake Mags said, her face a mask. She plopped the plastic bag down next to the items. "I'll be back." Without any other remarks, she left.

Charlotte stared at the items with longing. The only problem? They were about four feet out of reach.

Several minutes later, after taking off her sock and shoe, laying awkwardly on her side, and stretching her toes, she caught the edges of the plastic bag. Breathing heavily, she managed to pull the contents close enough to reach with her hands. Inside sat three containers. Charlotte opened each of them to reveal soup, some slices of apple, and a sandwich made of dry bread and what appeared to be a thin turkey slice.

Her first instinct was to devour everything in front of her, but Charlotte used all her willpower to resist. Once again, she didn't know if this would be the only food she got today and needed to ration it. Not to mention her stomach might cramp up if she ate too fast.

Seeing as how the soup would most likely be better hot, she chose that option first, sipping as she wondered how she'd reach the blanket bundle. It was about an extra foot out of reach from her longest stretch. The soup at least helped to warm her a little, but she knew from the howling wind outside and the lack of heat inside that mid-October weather in Boston would not be conducive to staying warm on a cold, concrete floor without extra help.

As she finished the last drops of soup, she reluctantly tucked away the apple slices and sandwich and stared at her predicament.

Then, suddenly, she laughed at the absurdity of her situation. How could she have possibly thought she would be safe proclaiming herself as the Messiah. Isabella had said she'd already fended off three attempts to kidnap Charlotte even before joining with her, Carla, and Jordan, Then, Charlotte basically created a giant target saying, "Come get me!" to any Triad out there who *didn't* want her to be the Messiah.

Luckily, this fake Mags and her accomplices didn't seem to want her dead, but if she couldn't get those blankets and clothes, she'd have a hard time making it through another night anyway.

Improvise, she told herself. *You can do this.*

Charlotte thought about what she had—plastic food containers with food, a plastic spoon, a plastic bag, and the clothes she had on.

My clothes... Charlotte examined herself. *Maybe...*

With slightly cramped fingers, she picked up her loose

running shoe. Tying the laces around the end of one of the plastic bag handles, she then used the other handle to flop the bag with the shoe attached towards the bundle. It landed on top, but she couldn't get it to pull the bundle forward. Taking off her other shoe, she tied that one to the first and lobbed the double-shoe while holding onto the bag's free handle. This time both shoes landed on the bundle, with one of them hanging slightly over the far edge. With delicate movements, she reeled in the bag. The bundle moved just a little bit.

Hope flared inside her tired chest. She repeated the movements over and over again until the gap was closed enough for her to reach it with her feet. She grabbed the edge of the bundle with her toes, and once more pulled the contents towards her. Wiggling out of her pants—which were still a touch moist from the briny liquid continually thrown in her face—she pulled on the dry sweatpants, new socks, and put her shoes on again. Stuffing the throw pillow under her sore butt, she then dragged both blankets over her cold, tired body. Without the cold seeping in through the floor and a buffer for the chilly air around her, Charlotte's body warmed up some after a few minutes.

Though a small victory, it was a victory nonetheless. With some food in her and a touch of warmth covering her, she leaned against one of the wide pipes behind her and nodded off.

Before she could fall into a deep enough sleep, she heard the door open again. Charlotte's exhausted eyelids resisted opening for a few moments. To her surprise, fake Mags didn't enter. Instead, three individuals came in. Two women and...

...a man.

Charlotte blinked a few times, registering the new additions to the room. Since the Triads touted an all-female line-up, so to speak, she'd never expected people working with them to be anything but women. Were there Triads out there that made exceptions to the Book's rules?

"She's younger than I thought," the first woman said. Her brown hair had been pulled tightly against her scalp into a skinny braid that hung over her shoulder. An accent tipped her words—Australian or New Zealand perhaps?

The second woman, whose short, black hair hung in a straight bob to the bottom of her chin peeked out underneath long bangs. "Not really what I expected, either." This one sounded straight out of Boston.

The man said nothing, merely bringing in a stool and placing it several feet from where Charlotte sat. He stared at her with his steely eyes, his chiseled jaw tight behind pressed closed lips. Underneath his other arm he carried a black rolled-up cloth.

Another blanket for me? Charlotte wondered. Apparently not as he moved behind Charlotte instead, unrolling the cloth in her peripheral view.

None of them spoke to her directly so, like with fake Mags, she didn't make any comments in return. She merely watched, noting any behavior which might help determine not only who these people were, but their rank in the group. Since none of them addressed her, she had a feeling they may be lackeys—not really supposed to "interact" with the prisoner. And since the man didn't speak at all, he was probably lowest on the proverbial totem pole.

Silence filled the space after a flapping noise indicated the man had finished setting up the cloth. Charlotte turned her head and saw the fabric hanging behind her, blocking the view of the pipes. Before she could think of its purpose, the brunette produced a recording device and placed it on the stool.

Ah, Charlotte thought. *They are making sure no one can see where I am when this recording takes place.* Automatically, she clung to the notion that these people wanted her alive. Too many thoughts of what other types of videos had been recorded where a person sat with a black cloth behind them flittered through her mind without her consent. Charlotte did her best to focus on something else, but fear crept up her spine like an icy centipede.

The black-haired woman pulled out a folded piece of paper from her pocket and tossed it into Charlotte's lap.

"Memorize this," she said. "If you don't, or if you stumble when you say the words, there will be consequences."

Charlotte picked up the piece of paper and unfolded it. Four paragraphs lay there in front of her, typed neatly on the page.

"Understand?" the woman asked again.

Charlotte nodded.

"Still don't get why we can't kill her."

The statement came from next to Charlotte. She started at the man's gruff voice. A little heated like fake Mags—a predator—as opposed to a cold, calculated declaration.

"C'mon mate," the brunette said, her accent thick. "You and Mae were always stoked at the thought of a little fun. You two are made for each other."

The man snorted a reply, finally taking his glare off Charlotte, and brusquely left the area.

Could it be? Fake Mags' name was Mae? It made sense, based on what had just been said. And, apparently, Mae and this man were romantically involved. So, there was more to this than Triads. This was a whole group, with personal connections as well.

The woman with the black hair spoke once again to Charlotte. "Someone will return later to record you. I'd start memorizing."

The two women walked away, their conversation too low for Charlotte to hear, and they exited quickly.

With a shaky sigh, Charlotte assessed what she could from the situation. She remembered Isabella once telling her that the reason she'd left her Triad had been because she'd discovered a file—a file that said some Triad members were recruiting *more* than just the three needed for their group and had started to form some sort of a cult.

Could this be what Charlotte had stumbled into? Not just one Triad with a few helpers, but a large group which had been enlisting many others?

But to what end? And why set the fires?

Too many questions rolled around in her mind. Instead, she smoothed the paper and began to read what they wanted her to say.

The words on the page surprised her. As she read, she understood more and more. They'd tailored it so well, pulling on most things she would already say, but adding in a few others to create their own fabricated story.

She knew what they were planning to do.

But even more than that, she knew they'd made a mistake...

15

October 18th
6:30 p.m.

Sean took the stairs to his apartment two at a time, carrying a pizza in one hand and his keys in the other. He could hardly believe how tired and hungry he felt, and yet it made sense. This had been the third day since the APB went out on Mags for murdering Juliette. The precinct hadn't made any real progress, and now that Sean knew of her connection to the Triads, he didn't believe their chances of ever finding her were very high.

Millan's meeting hadn't gone any better. Their new sergeant would be arriving on Monday to be "shown the ropes" of their precinct. No other information had been given about their incoming new boss except they were transferring in from Portland, Oregon. Millan had also requested the announcement about his retirement still not be made until Monday.

Sean hadn't been a fan of that plan, since not only would there be a new boss in everyone's face, but also because that day contained Juliette's funeral. The whole situation in general left him reeling and he already knew about the upcoming change. He couldn't imagine the rest of the precinct's reaction to the news, sprung on them on such a somber day.

Millan's face had seemed even more haggard as the days of the week had gone by and during the meeting, Sean noted the bloodshot look in his eyes and a stoop to his shoulders. Sean knew the retiring man blamed himself for so many things, ever since the Triad trial ended a week ago. Since then, their murder suspect had been found not guilty, escaped, then was killed during a mugging; the defense attorney who'd been secretly sending Sean messages had been murdered at her apartment; Millan's wife had threatened to leave him, and now the whole Mags fiasco.

Sean couldn't blame the man for wanting to bail, but at the same time he'd been angry at him. They were all trying to stick together through this as a team. Millan's team. How many more members could they lose before their group was no longer recognizable?

Yet how much had the team already changed?

In the meantime, the precinct hopped onto every possible tip about Mags, with officers running around the city like maniacs. Sean hadn't even had time to have lunch and he'd thought about staying late to catch up on paperwork, but then received a message from Elaine, telling him she could arrive for their meeting a little earlier than seven.

He'd somehow completely forgotten about Woods staying at his place and Elaine joining up with the two of them that evening. Instead of dealing with the mountain of paperwork on his desk, Sean changed tactics and spent his last hour searching for the contact information on the websites he'd said he would do.

Afterwards, he left work, with the names and addresses of the website owners now logged into his phone, sitting snugly in his pocket. Finally at the top of the stairs of his building, he entered his apartment.

The room looked like a bomb had hit it.

Placing the pizza quickly on the ground next to the open door, Sean pulled his weapon and entered slowly. A quick glance to the right and he saw Woods in his kitchen, pouring soda into a glass. Two boxes of delivery food sat open on the countertop next to him.

Lowering his gun with an exhale, Sean said, "What the hell went on in here, man?"

Woods held his hand up in an apology. "I couldn't sit still. Come, see what I've put together."

Now that his adrenaline started to drain, Sean took in the sight of his studio apartment a little more clearly. Papers were strewn all over the coffee table, arms of the couch, and floor—some in small piles, some fanned out, some by themselves. The wall straight ahead from the door had been covered with pictures and smaller bits of paper hung up by tape. A whiteboard was jammed into the corner on the left between the window and the television set. On it were multiple scribbles, more pictures and papers, and questions written haphazardly around them all.

Woods moved to the wall first. "I started here, putting together everything I could remember. Then I went to the library and printed out the files I had on my flash drive, since I couldn't recoup the ones destroyed in the fire. Luckily, I'd gotten into the habit of always keeping a backup on me, just in case." He moved to the whiteboard, his eyes wide. "But there was too much to print, and I ran out of cash. So, I stopped at an office supply store and picked up a few more items. I think I'm noticing a pattern here, but I became stuck, so I ordered Chinese food to give my mind a rest while waiting for you to return."

A deep breath was the only thing that stopped the Brit from continuing his rant. With an abrupt twist, he turned to Sean. "Have you heard anything about the rest of my team?"

Sean finally grabbed the pizza from outside in the hallway and finished entering the apartment, his mind spinning.

"Uh...sorry, no. I didn't get a chance to check in with the Fire Department, but Elaine said she'd look into it and let us know when she got here tonight. She should be here soon." He paused, noticing that Woods now wore different clothes than the night before. "You didn't go back to your hotel, did you?"

Woods shook his head, running a hand over his dark, shaven scalp. A very thin layer of black stubble had begun to appear. "No, of course not. I stopped at a department store and a chemist's before I went to the library."

"Chemist's?" Sean asked, unfamiliar with the term.

"Apologies. Pharmacy." He gestured towards the bathroom. "I couldn't handle my own breath this morning. Figured I should remedy that."

Sean smiled at the tension-breaker. "I brought pizza. Didn't know if you'd eaten."

"I'm all right for now. Thoughtful of you, though."

Sean plopped the box onto the kitchen counter since there was no room on the coffee table for much of anything else. He snagged a piece and bit in. This time he'd gone with buffalo chicken and green peppers and the spices mixed with the cheese caused his tastebuds to tingle with joy. He promised himself not to skip lunch anymore—a promise he'd made many times during his life and often broken.

Before he could do much of anything else except enjoy the moment, the intercom to his apartment sounded.

"Mush be Ewaine," he said through a full mouth. He hit the talk button, heard her voice, and buzzed her in. A few moments later, all three of them stood gathered in his place.

"Intros," Sean said, wiping his mouth quickly with a napkin. "Elaine McDuffall, meet Inspector Omani Woods. Elaine is a journalist with a local news station. She spotted arson patterns and connected them with the Triads. Woods, here, is from Interpol in Britain, though technically he's operating off their radar. He and his team have been working for a few years now on Triad-related incidents and recently connected it to the arsons, which have been occurring outside the U.S. as well." Sean waved his hand at them and stuffed more pizza into his mouth.

The two of them shook hands and Woods gestured for her

to sit on the couch.

"Interpol, huh?" Elaine asked as she moved.

Sean could hear the eager journalist in her tone. But just as quickly he noted the sparkle leave her eyes. She understood, just like they all did, that this was not a story to be told on the news.

Mostly they needed to work together so no one else died.

Woods moved aside some papers to clear a space for her.

"Looks like you two have been busy," she said, motioning to the clutter, wall, and whiteboard.

"That's all been Woods," Sean said after swallowing a large chunk of chicken. "I just got here from work a few minutes ago."

"Well, no time like the present." Elaine flipped her hair and yanked the shoulder-length bag she carried onto her lap. From inside, she pulled several folders, all colored differently, and placed them next to her on the couch. "I figure the best course of action is for each of us to discuss what we've learned so far about both the Triads and the arson cases. I'm sure some of our information will overlap, but I think it's better not to interrupt each other, even if we already have heard the material. Hearing the details more than once could be helpful." She tilted her head for a moment as if thinking. "I'm sure there will be a lot of data. This may take a while."

Sean bristled for about half a second at her taking control of the situation, but then shrugged the feeling off. He worked best when he could fit pieces together, not organize information. Besides, this way he could eat more pizza while the other two went first.

One thing did pop into his head though and he interrupted Elaine. "Before we start, what did you find out about the office building fire?"

Woods stiffened at the question, his brow furrowed.

"Oh yeah," she said, pulling out a different file from her knapsack, this one a plain manilla folder.

For work, Sean thought. This way she wouldn't confuse her news stories with the stuff about the Triads.

"Let's see..." she muttered before speaking up. "Preliminary reports do suggest arson. There was an accelerant on site—acetone—which appeared to have been placed inside two barrels in a storage closet on the fourth floor. The blast took out the front entrance of the room, the north-facing side of that floor, plus did damage to the two floors above. Most of the building was empty for the day, thank goodness, but there were still about thirty people left inside. Two casualties on the fourth floor in the main fire area. Nasty, those. And three injured from the sixth floor—mostly bumps and bruises. They worked for...some kind of public relations company. The group on the fourth floor, with the deaths, was—"

"We know," Sean said, interrupting her casual remarks. He nodded over to Woods.

She glanced over at him. "What am I missing?"

"I was operating from that floor. With my team," Woods said, the words tight. "We set up the office under a dummy name."

A look of embarrassment crossed Elaine's face. "I didn't...I wasn't," she said, stumbling over her words.

Sean waved her concern away. "I forgot to tell you it was Woods' people, so you couldn't have known. In fact, no one knows about his setup there, except those of us in this room."

Woods perked up. "You said there were only two bodies found deceased?"

Elaine checked her notes. "Yes, male and female. No ID's as of yet."

"Wasn't there another team member?" Sean asked. "Four of you total?"

A vigorous nod accompanied Woods' next words. "Yes. Maybe Leeds or Franks got out? We should check their hotels, see if they returned."

Sean held up a hand. Something gnawed at the edges of his mind. He recalled the previous night when he'd arrived at the office building. Woods had been outside, having a cigarette. "Woods, you said you'd given up smoking, right?"

Another furrowed brow at the change in subject. "Yes."

"And your team believed that?"

"Yes. Where are you going with this?"

"Give me a second. Did you tell them you were going out to smoke?"

"No. I said I was going to pop into the loo. I even left my coat. Didn't want anyone to know. I was...embarrassed that I'd picked up the habit once again."

"That means they, your team, thought you'd still be on the same floor. The fourth floor?"

Woods shrugged. "I suppose so."

Elaine's eyes widened as if following Sean's logic. "So, a different one of them wasn't there during the explosion, but *that person* thought you'd be there with the others on the fourth floor."

"Exactly," Sean replied.

"I don't follow," Woods replied.

Sean hesitated for a moment. He understood how hard his next statement may be for Woods to hear. "The culprit had to know what floor your team was on, ignite the incendiary device, have enough time to get out, and know all of you would be there at that specific time."

"Yes...and...?"

"Whoever didn't die in that fire must be the perpetrator. Only they could confirm the presence of the rest of the team. So, if only one person wasn't killed, it must have been either...who did you say? Oh yeah, Leeds or Franks."

Several moments of tense silence passed. "It can't be..." Woods said under his breath. He sunk onto the couch. "I vetted both those women myself. They were clean."

Sean felt his pain. When he'd realized Mags had killed Juliette... except it wasn't Mags. Could one of Woods' team members be a fake Triad persona, too?

Too many tangents. "Look, Elaine is right. Before we start searching for any conclusions, each of us should go through what we know. There are too many variables to deal with. Once we have everything out in the open, I know the pieces will start to come together and some of this will begin to make sense. It has to." Sean said these last few words more quietly, but he could see the heaviness revolving around this situation reflected in the eyes of his two companions. They'd all lost people close to them as well—and fairly recently—so he knew they wanted some closure, whatever that may look like, just as he did.

And Sean had a feeling it would get messier before it made

sense.

"Elaine?" he continued. "Go ahead and start."

Elaine began slowly, a bit tentative compared to her normal gusto, but eventually she got into a rhythm. She revealed the specifics about her work on the Triad trial, how she'd discovered Charlotte and Mags had traveled around the world pursuing a "list of addresses" that could be connected to other Triad activity, and how she'd followed up on two of those addresses in Vermont. Though these places were recently vacated, she found nearby locations filled with new tenants around the time the Triad bunker had been found.

"With Sean's help," she continued, "we checked out these two places. They'd been set on fire and the inhabitants killed." She paused and Sean knew what she was about to say next. "A journalist who was helping me had been staking out one of the locations—a lake house. Whoever set the fire used her car, with her inside it, to ram the house and explode." Elaine swallowed, hard, and Sean could see tears form in her eyes.

"My condolences," Woods said.

Elaine gave a weak smile, then went on, as if talking helped her stay focused. "Anyway, after that Sean and I decided to look over the rest of the address list—you know, from when Charlotte and Mags traveled the world—and to check for the same kind of arson cases around those listed. Three nights ago, on Tuesday, we'd planned to head out to Keene, New Hampshire to check out the next set of addresses. Except that was the night..." She trailed off.

"That was the night Detective Tay was murdered," Sean finished for her.

Elaine cleared her throat. "As you can imagine, things got busy and complicated, so the trip didn't pan out. But in the meantime, I have been monitoring online sites that have to do with the Triads. A bunch have popped up in the past six months—since everything first went down in that bunker. But two sites caught my interest: one referenced Triads from *before* the big bunker blowout and the second had an audio clip of a woman claiming herself to be the Messiah of the Triads."

Another several moments of silence as all this information was ingested by Woods.

"Impressive," he finally said. "It appears you've discovered quite a lot on your own. There are definitely fragments in there that help answer some questions, as well as allow for some possible leads."

"Like what?" Elaine asked.

"Hold on," Sean said. "Let him fill us in on the evidence he's gathered, first, before we focus on only one piece of information."

A slight pout touched her mouth.

"This was your plan," he reminded her.

The look vanished in an instant. "Of course, of course. Please, continue," she said to Woods.

Sean couldn't help but notice the brief eye contact from Woods to himself. He felt like the Brit was also a touch irritated by the young woman. Still, in Sean's mind, what she lacked in maturity she made up for in tenacity. And she kind of grew on a person.

Woods began gesturing to different parts of the apartment—from the wall to the whiteboard to the coffee table. He told them he'd been working on the possibility of other Triads for a little over three years, how he'd investigated mysterious circumstances in multiple other countries, and how the Triad trial in Boston and the fires he'd been tracking the past six months finally connected everything together.

"My main goal," he went on, "was to determine if these fires are to cover up Triad activity or expose it. The attacks are coordinated, but the fires themselves are sloppy, leading me to believe there is a form of leadership giving orders, but that those carrying out these orders may be amateurs. At that point, I recruited Detective Tay to help. I believed her profiling skills and personal experience with a Triad group would prove invaluable. She created a profile of the arsonist, though she believed the attacks must be caused by a group of people instead of an individual, which we considered as well. Detective Tay said she thought the arson strikes were personal—a message or punishment against these Triad groups." He gave a slight grimace. "Unfortunately, I spent very little time with her to follow up on her assessment before..."

Sean felt a lump form in his throat.

"We also discovered the fires which occurred in Vermont," Woods continued, nodding to Elaine. "But there are two things of note you didn't mention. Sean told us that, one, the occupant of the lake house didn't die in the fire. She'd actually struck her head on the dock outside and drowned. The coroner put the time of death a few hours before the fire."

Elaine started. "What? Sean, why didn't you tell me that?"

Sean rubbed his face. "Didn't I? Sorry, I thought—"

"Ugh. This is what happens when you aren't organized,"

she murmured, pushing the laundry basket next to the couch closer to the wall.

Sean ground his teeth. He'd been quite preoccupied that week to remember every little detail. Even if he'd been organized, he assumed he'd told her, and he was starting to tire of her inconsiderate attitude. "Listen—"

"And two," Woods continued loudly, cutting Sean off, most likely to stave off an argument, "is that a witness claims to have seen two dark-haired women leave the house in separate cars. One of them may have been Mags."

Sean creased his forehead, recalling the timeline of the lake house fire. "It couldn't have been Mags. She'd been in the hospital, visiting Payne when he woke up. Juliette even picked her up around the time the fire would have been set."

Woods paused, a hint of anger in his flared nostrils. "I didn't realize that. So, does that indicate it was two different women? This does confirm that there are a group of them and not just a single arsonist."

Elaine added, "And, whoever it was, it really seems as if these fires are well planned, but sloppily executed. That lends well to your "amateur theory."

Sean wanted to dig deeper but shook his head. "Woods, why don't you finish what you know. We can return to all these threads later."

With a nod, Woods went on, his expression once again neutral. "My interest in the Triads first began when I received a case revolving around a woman I'd caught who'd killed a neighbor. While in custody, the woman babbled on about a Book and that her team would come and get her—that she was invaluable as a third. I had no clue what it meant at the time. When I went a week later to visit her in her holding cell to ask a few more questions about case details, she appeared to be an entirely different woman. I mean, she looked the same, but her demeanor, vocabulary, even mannerisms were all distinct. I didn't really think much of it at the time, merely noting it in the case file, before moving on.

"Two weeks before her trial," he continued, "I heard she'd wound up dead. Killed by food poisoning so severe she burst something inside her esophagus and bled to death. For whatever reason, her death nagged at me, nibbling at me like a fox. I pressed the issue, watching old videos of the woman's pre-trial, and was astounded by the difference between the time I'd arrested her and her appearances after that. She claimed she didn't know what crime we were accusing her of and had no recollection of even being arrested."

Sean recognized the pattern. He'd seen the same evidence in Angellica. Could Woods understand that he'd basically been dealing with two different women?

"Nothing came from it," Woods said, sitting on the arm of the couch, "until about six months later. I received an anonymous call from a woman who told me to check out a case in France. She claimed it was related to the case with the poisoned accused murderer. I followed her recommendation, curious, and met up with Detective De'leu."

Again, Sean recognized the name. He'd met the man on the fourth floor of the building that had blown up. *French*, he thought, *with a big nose.* Sean didn't know why that detail mattered anymore, but it just sort of popped in there. *So many deaths—so many people where these Triad women snuffed them out as if their lives meant nothing.*

Woods went on. "De'leu had encountered a female suspect who claimed amnesia about the murder she'd committed. When I pressed him for details, De'leu told me he felt something was 'off' when he went to visit her for questioning. He told me she seemed...different. As if, even though she appeared the same, she'd become someone else."

"And that's how it started," Sean said. "Your pursuit of the Triads."

Woods nodded. "After that, I became obsessed. I didn't know anything about 'Triads' at that point, but I did recognize a pattern emerging. I got other agents involved. Looked for anything unusual." He then explained how he'd met up with Simone in Lyon, France about the pre-Sumerian pages she'd been sent anonymously and about Agent Tam from Hong Kong who'd talked about a case involving a woman claiming she didn't want to be the "savior" or "Messiah" of the three women she'd killed.

"So there had been another Messiah, or at least someone who claimed to be one," Elaine said, her eyes lighting up.

"It seems so. And now, as you've discovered, a new woman is claiming this title again," Woods finished.

Sean bit his tongue. He knew keeping Charlotte's name out of things was stupid. The three of them needed to know everything in order to stop these arsonists and find Charlotte at all. But for some reason, he couldn't do it. The idea of implicating her without more knowledge about why she'd declared herself as Messiah seemed illogical. And he knew, deep down, that whatever her reasoning, she was trying to do good.

"I guess that means you're up, Sean," Elaine said, shifting her body towards him.

Sean hadn't fully decided about how much he wanted to tell them. He held so many secrets it was hard to keep track of what to share and what to keep quiet. But before he could say anything, his door intercom buzzed. He glanced over at the two of them. "Either of you expecting anyone?"

They both shook their heads.

Sean made his way over and opened the communication. "Hello?" he asked.

"Hey. It's Pay—."

Per usual, the system cut off while the person spoke, but Sean recognized the voice.

It was his partner, Detective Payne.

16

October 18th
7:00 p.m.

Charlotte willed her hands to stop shaking as the door opened. She'd spent the last several hours reciting, very under her breath, the words given to her for her upcoming "speech." While she'd practiced, she'd noticed a second small issue with the words laid out to her and hoped no one else would notice. Not sure exactly how she could use it to her advantage—or perhaps the mistake had been done on purpose—but any inconsistencies on the part of this arson group should be examined thoroughly for exploitation possibilities.

For now, though, all she could do was hope she didn't make a mistake while performing under duress.

Fake Mags, or Mae as she could now call her, strolled in.

"You ready?" she asked, that same sly grin on her face.

Charlotte nodded.

"Better run the speech by me first. Won't hurt to use your voice a bit, too, while we wait for the others to show up."

As soon as Charlotte opened her mouth to begin, the two women and man who'd set up the room from before entered.

"Guess there won't be time to practice," Mae said, hissing the words under her breath. She leaned over, inches from Charlotte's face. "Better not fuck it up." Venom coated the sentence. She straightened and greeted the new additions to the room. The man walked right up to Mae and put a hand on her waist.

"Hey, babe," he said.

Mae's grin widened, as though she'd like to devour him in a lustful way. "Hey, yourself."

"The words of lovebirds," the Australian woman said in a mocking tone. "How cute."

"Flowery crap wastes time." Mae sucked at her teeth. "Takes away from other things. Now pure passion..." In a flash she was kissing the man, their tongues entwined as if breathing were only an option and not a necessity.

The black-haired woman tutted. "Enough, already you two. You'll have plenty of time for that later. We got to get this done, fast."

Mae pulled away, the look in her eyes one of triumph—the look in his of adoration.

Power dynamic between the two of them? Charlotte wondered.

They each helped set up the lighting, removing all the items around Charlotte to make sure none of them showed in the frame. Luckily, Charlotte had finished the sandwich and apple pieces a while ago since all her possessions were dumped unceremoniously on the dirty floor near the far wall. After clearing the area, they all moved away towards the door and stood still, except the Aussie who sat crouched behind the stool, peering through the recording device.

No one moved or gave any orders.

Charlotte raised her eyebrows.

"One minute," Mae told her, answering her unvoiced question.

Suddenly, the gurgling and hissing pipes around her stopped. The lack of constant sounds in the background she'd been listening to for two days put her on edge.

"All right. Let's do this."

They do not want any noise, Charlotte thought. *They are worried about someone finding this location. Finding me before they are finished using me. At least that means they either a) plan to keep me alive longer or b) plan to continue to use this location. Only (a) really helps me, though.*

Mae spoke once more. "Remember, every time you mess up the lines, there will be consequences. So, I advise you to get it right. Don't try any delaying crap. Understood?"

Charlotte nodded.

After a couple more minutes, the recording device showed a red light and the black-haired woman pointed at Charlotte to begin.

With a deep breath, and hoping her voice sounded steady,

she began her recitation:

"Triad members. This is the Messiah speaking. I'm here, as promised, to deliver on a new path for all of us. This path may not be easy to understand, but it's the best course of action. As the Messiah, I'm ordering it, and it will be so.

"This new path," she continued, "will allow the Triad members to finally be at peace. In our world, we have succeeded in attaining our goals. We've done what the Book set out for us to do. It's now our time to cease all hostile acts and retire the concept of the Triads as a whole.

"I understand that this path isn't easy for many of you to hear. Those who resist will meet with the same fate as any who disobey my orders. You have heard of the fires. You have heard of the Coalition. They are under my rule to dispose of any Triad members who don't follow my orders.

"You can't stay hidden. I already know your locations. If you stop your Triad activity, the Coalition will leave you be. You'll be able to live out your lives normally. But if you resist, we will find you. It's my duty to enforce the guidelines I've set out for you. Follow my lead and you'll be free from Triad rule and free from the Coalition."

Charlotte ended the monologue and the recording device deactivated.

"Looks good on my end," the black-haired woman said. "Sent."

Mae simply stared; her eyes narrowed. Charlotte didn't know if the woman hoped she'd mess up or wondered why

Charlotte hadn't fought reciting the message.

The group removed the lighting, pulled down the black cloth from behind her, and returned the blankets and such to Charlotte's area. Mae simply stood the whole time, watching.

"Come on, babe, let's go," the man said to Mae.

"In a minute, Patrick. I want to check on something."

Patrick gave her shoulder a squeeze, then left.

Once the door closed behind him, Mae spoke.

"What did we miss?" she asked.

Charlotte cleared her throat. "What do you mean?"

"Don't play games. You seemed too okay with that speech. I didn't notice any pauses or sighs or throat swallowing. You talked like you didn't care you were saying those things. Why?"

Charlotte hesitated for a moment. She could either feign ignorance—though she believed Mae might see through it regardless—or try and create a wedge between her and other members of the group.

She chose the latter.

"Did it not seem odd to you that the speech had me claiming control over the Coalition?"

Charlotte could see Mae trying to figure out what she meant. "It's part of our plan.

"It is part of *someone's* plan, but not yours. Someone who actually commands the Coalition but is not a direct part of it."

"What makes you say that?"

"Ask your boss about the fate of the Coalition when I am no longer around."

This time, Mae's brow furrowed. "What does that have to do with anything?"

"If I claimed myself as Messiah and the fires are occurring under my orders, what happens when I am dead? Unless you plan on keeping me around and using me as a continued 'Messiah,' which for some reason, I do not believe." Charlotte had to tread very carefully. She didn't want to push Mae too far.

"And why's that?"

"Because the Messiah cannot die."

"Yeah, so?"

Charlotte shook her head as if disappointed. "I am surprised at someone so smart who cannot see what is right in front of her."

Mae stepped over quickly and smacked Charlotte across the face. The sting reached all the way up from her jawbone to her earlobe and the room spun for a moment.

"You'll tell me exactly what I want to know, or you'll pay for it. And you will *never* insult me like that again."

Charlotte closed her eyes for a moment, lifted her chin, then stared squarely at Mae. "You have all the information you need." She held her gaze.

Mae raised her hand again and Charlotte tightened up her face, though she didn't flinch away. But the blow never came. Instead, Mae lowered her hand slowly, a grin spreading across her face.

"I know you. I've studied you. This won't be the way to get to you, to make you behave. But I know the way. A nice, sweet, cute detective you like so damn much."

Sean. Charlotte's heart raced. *Keep it together*, she told herself.

"I'll bring him here so you can watch. You know what I'm

capable of. You may not be able to be permanently damaged, but there's no restrictions on him. Clear?"

Charlotte gave the tiniest nod in understanding. "I do not know everything," she said. "But two things are apparent. If your group wanted to keep me alive indefinitely as a fake Messiah, they could have done so easily, without all this pomp and circumstance. I *planned* to tell the Triads to stop. But I did not know about the Coalition until now. Your group knew enough about how I would proceed with the Triads for plausibility, but someone added my control over the arsonists. The question is, why?"

Mae didn't respond, but Charlotte could see her jaw tighten.

"And the second thing?" Mae asked.

"Whoever wrote that speech did so to prove that I was being coerced into speaking. To what end, I do not know."

"What do you mean? There's nothing in it to show you didn't mean what you were saying."

"It is not *what* I was saying, but *how* I said it."

Mae's eyes flitted back and forth, searching internally for the problem. Suddenly, they lit up. "Contractions. You don't fucking use contractions."

Charlotte gave a nod of agreement.

"But why? Why would she set this up this way?"

She? So, there is one woman behind all this. "I am not sure. All I know, is, whoever is orchestrating this is setting me up to appear fake or coerced *and* establishing the Coalition to be connected to me."

Mae rocked on her heels, her gaze drifting around the

room. "She wouldn't..." she murmured.

Charlotte remained quiet, silently urging a fracture of faith to be created inside Mae's mind. If this woman could doubt her boss, or the plan...

Suddenly, as if remembering where she was, Mae's stare snapped once again to Charlotte. "I'll have some food brought in," she said. "And another bottle of water."

Charlotte merely nodded, her stomach tightening in anticipation.

Mae turned to leave, but there was less swagger in her walk.

No matter what Mae believed, the conversation had obviously shaken her. And a shaken prisoner guard was one that might make a mistake.

Or become an ally...

17

October 18ᵗʰ
7:30 p.m.

"Payne?" Sean asked through the apartment's intercom. "What are you doing here?"

"I tried to c— you, but you didn't answer. Thought may— something had happened. Called the pre— and they told me about your crappy cell serv— so I thought I'd stop by. I brought so— beer and thought we c— chat about Mags' case. Can— come up?"

Sean glanced at Elaine and Woods. "It's my partner," he told them.

"Does he know about the Triads?" Woods asked.

"Nothing more than what was on the news. He wasn't

working in Boston yet during the bunker stuff six months ago—just the trial. But he's never mentioned anything about the Triads outside of the normal 'crazy women killing people' remarks."

Elaine chimed in. "You can't let him up. He can't know about this stuff. It'll just put him in danger."

"Plus, he can't know I'm staying here," Woods added. "He'll have to report it."

The intercom buzzed again.

"Okay, okay. I'll go down and deal with him." Sean told Payne he'd be right there. While descending the two flights of stairs, he wondered how he could get rid of him. Sean could lie and say he had Charlotte over, but he didn't want Payne mentioning that to someone either. The two of them hadn't discussed going public with their relationship.

Not that it matters, he said, jumping the last two stairs. *She's involved with the Triads and being held prisoner somewhere in a warehouse. And I have no way to help her or find her or...*

Sean forced these unhelpful thoughts from his mind as he opened the outside door.

"Hey," he said, letting Payne into the main downstairs area and out of the cold.

"I know I shouldn't have just shown up like this," Payne said, blowing on his free hand, "but like I told you, you weren't answering your phone and I wanted to work on this Mags thing with you. Off the books, of course." He held up a six pack.

"Normally, I would. The problem is, I have company over."

Payne raised an eyebrow. "Company?"

"Nothing like that. Just a couple people I know. So, it's really not a good time."

A grinding noise issued from Payne's jaw. "I get it. It's just...I'm having a hard time waiting. I need to be doing something."

Sean thought about how he'd feel if the situation were reversed, and Charlotte had killed someone. "I get it, I really do. But tonight won't work."

Payne narrowed his eyes. "I can't just sit around and wait."

"I'm not asking you to. Do whatever you have to but talking with me right now isn't it. Sorry, man."

Payne lowered the beer and a steely look settled over him. "The district attorney from the Triad trial is dead."

The words took a minute to sink in. "Jordan Parker?" Sean recalled chatting with the Southern woman in preparation for his cross-examination.

Payne nodded. "I've been listening in on the police scanner. She was found in her apartment last night, outside of our jurisdiction so none of our team knows about it. Half the place was torched, but it looked like the fire was extinguished before it flamed her up. Wouldn't have mattered anyway. She'd been stabbed three times first."

Sean shook his head, trying to figure out why this was so important that it couldn't wait a day to talk about. "Okay, that's awful, but I don't get why you care about this."

"A woman matching Mags' description was seen fleeing the scene by a neighbor."

Shock coursed through him. Mags, or this Mae person,

was still running around killing? Even with the whole city after her? What was she thinking? Or did she want to get caught?

A dull throb began behind his eyes. He had to steer Payne off this subject. He couldn't handle another person getting caught up in this. "Okay, okay. That's not good. But the witness could have been wrong. You're reinstated to work after the weekend, right?"

"Yeah."

"We can contact the other precinct and ask them about the case then, find out about the witness, etcetera."

"Fine. But I'm looking into the D.A., see why she might have been a target."

Sean's head swam. "You do that. We'll talk more on Monday."

"Thanks, Trann. I appreciate that you're on my side about this." He pulled off a beer and tossed it over to Sean.

Sean caught the drink then waved him off, not sure what else to say. Payne had no idea what he was getting himself into, and the less he knew, the safer he would be.

With slow steps, Sean headed back upstairs. Before he went in, he took in a deep breath. Things were getting more and more complicated. The district attorney? She'd been part of the Triad trial, sure, but was that enough to kill her?

Sean remembered that the defense attorney had also been murdered, but only because she'd been secretly sending Sean texts warning him about her client. Had Jordan stumbled upon something she shouldn't have? Something related to the Triads that the Triads found out about, so they had her killed?

Deaths were piling up. New pieces kept adding to this

insane puzzle. And Sean knew he could figure it out, but he wasn't sure if he could keep Charlotte's name and Mags' email out of the picture anymore. With Woods' and Elaine's information, the path seemed clearer, but there were still too many missing cogs to make the mechanism work.

Sean reentered his apartment, closing the door behind him.

"That took a while," Elaine said. She'd apparently made some space on the table for her folders. Sean could hear Woods washing his hands in the bathroom from behind the door. A moment later, he emerged.

"That was my partner, Payne. He's convinced Mags isn't a killer and wanted to go over theories with me."

"Does he know she's involved with the Triads?" Woods asked. He'd unbuttoned the top button on his dress shirt. Sean knew his apartment could run pretty hot—radiator heating wasn't always exact.

"I don't think so," Sean answered. "I think he's just in denial." Sean realized he still held the beer from Payne in his hand. He debated cracking it open and chugging it as fast as possible. He wanted to take the edge off this whole situation, but the rational part of him decided a clear head would be better. He could drink before he passed out later. Or, possibly, to *help* him pass out later.

Woods crossed his arms, his face pensive. "I have another theory. About Mags. But it may be a little out there."

"Hold on," Elaine said. "Sean needs to share his info first."

"Wait," Sean said. "This may have relevance to my stuff. Go ahead."

Elaine flipped her hair and scowled, disapprovingly.

"Well, I remembered going through the files from the Triad trial. Detective Tay had emailed me a copy of them. I found myself intrigued by the idea that the woman on trial got off on an insanity plea."

"Oh yeah," Elaine added. She straightened, almost as if reporting the news. "Apparently because of drug use, behavioral modification, and brainwashing, the jury ruled she wasn't in a fit state of mind during her involvement with the other women in the bunker."

Woods stared at Sean. "You saw her shoot and kill a coworker..."

"Officer Eth," Sean said, filling in the name. A dryness overtook his throat. Another loss to these Triad women.

"You testified that the defendant killed him."

"Yes."

Woods cocked his head. "What did you think of the insanity plea? Did it hold weight, based on what you saw on the scene?"

Here it was. The moment of truth. If Sean told them what he really believed, he'd have to reveal everything to prove he was right. That Mags wasn't really Mags. But if they *didn't* believe him, this would end their joint venture. He couldn't continue to work with them if they thought he was nuts.

You have to find out, he said. *If they can't accept it, you shouldn't work with them anymore anyway because they'll be looking in the wrong direction. You gotta do it.*

"All right. I'm going to go through all my stuff and then you can ask whatever you want at the end. But what I'm about to say will make or break this group. Either you believe me, or you don't. So here goes."

Sean spoke for about twenty minutes, letting out everything he knew. He started with Angellica, about learning of the Triad group in the bunker. Then, how other Triads were talked about and how evidence pointed to their continued presence. He told them about his interviews with the bunker women, his happiness when Mags and Charlotte returned without any evidence that other Triads existed, and then his disappointment when Elaine showed up with fresh information.

"Well, I'm sorry, but—" Elaine said in a huff.

"Let him continue," Woods interrupted, gently but firmly.

"I didn't want anything more to do with Triads," Sean explained. "They'd kidnapped Mags and Tay, shot Tay and me, and left Charlotte for dead." He inhaled deeply. "But the main reason I didn't want them to really exist was for Charlotte's sake. They claimed her as their Messiah." He glanced over at Elaine and watched as her facial expression changed from confusion to realization.

"So, when you came to me," he said to Elaine, "I kept Charlotte in the dark. I didn't want to risk putting her in danger if I didn't have to. Except, I think, she's doing the same thing for me."

"It's her. On that audio clip, isn't it?" Elaine's eyes glinted with greed.

Sean's jaw clenched for a few moments before he replied. "I think so, yes."

Elaine's eyes turned dark. "You kept that from me. After

everything I told you!"

"I did. And I'd do it again."

The words came out so plainly that Elaine had nothing to say in reply.

"I didn't know how she was involved," he went on. "Coerced, drugged, or undercover maybe? And after what happened with Mags, I worried she'd be seen as just another criminal to add to the APB.

"But—!" he said, stifling Elaine's next words, "I recently learned she's in danger. She's been taken and is being held at a warehouse somewhere. Whatever her level of involvement, right now she's in trouble."

Woods nodded, knowingly. "You did not report this to your team at the precinct."

"You two are the only people who know."

Elaine frowned. "Except...except how did you find out about her predicament? Someone else must know. Someone told you or you overhead a conversation?"

You've come this far...

"Okay. Here comes the crazy-sounding part."

"Trann," Woods said. "We're here discussing multiple arsons based on groups of Triad women around the world. I'm fairly certain whatever you have to say, we'll be open to it."

Sean nodded. "I learned about Charlotte's situation... from Mags."

Silence coated the room. Elaine's face portrayed shock while Woods' looked angry.

"You know where that murderer is?" Woods asked, fury tainting his words.

"No. I don't. I swear. I received a message from her this morning, sent to my work email. It deleted itself after about ten minutes. I didn't have time to trace it and she didn't reveal her location."

"Why didn't you tell me?" Woods demanded.

"Because it's not Mags who's doing all this," Sean said.

"Just because she's your friend—"

Elaine placed a hand lightly on the Brit's arm. "Let him finish," she said.

Sean continued. "You asked me about the woman at the Triad trial. Violet."

Woods' forehead creased. "You mean Veronica. Right? Wasn't her name Veronica?"

Sean cleared his throat. "I saw Violet kill Detective Eth. When I showed up in that courtroom, the woman in that chair was *not* Violet."

"Temporary insanity," Woods said. "Correct?"

Sean shook his head. "No. It wasn't her. It was Veronica."

"I do not understand..."

"I didn't really either. Not at first. I'd seen it with my ex. She really was two different people. And then I'd remembered what Angellica, well when she was Anya, told me in the bunker. Half the crap she talked about wasn't true, but some of it was. I'd planned to chat with those bunker women again at some point to get more answers but...you know...everything happened with Juliette and Mags.

"Anyway," he went on, "Anya mentioned that the 're-programming' the Triads did targeted the psychopathic and sociopathic tendencies in their subject and removed them. She said the alternate persona, Angellica, was really her, but without those tendencies. Then, they added in the rest of their 'fake' lives with false memories to fill in any past gaps."

"And you believe this was done to Mags?" Woods asked.

"I do. And if it's true, Mags is the person she should be, but Mae is the way she was born."

"Mae?" Elaine asked.

"In the email, that's what Mags called her alter-ego."

Another bout of quiet.

"Let me see if I am getting everything," Woods said. "You've been in contact with the woman who killed a team member of yours, who possibly set fire to *my* team, and is being hunted by every law enforcement office in Boston as we speak."

"No," Sean said, stressing the word. "I've been in contact with *Mags*. She is not the criminal here."

"But she exists in the same body as this...Mae."

"Yeah."

Woods let out a soft snort. "I was mistaken. This is, as you put it, 'crazy-sounding.'"

Sean paced in his kitchen, Payne's lone beer on the counter looking better and better as a headache started to form at the base of his skull. "Look, I get it. Trust me. But what do we already believe? Groups of murderous women around the world. A worldwide organized arson group." Sean tugged on his ear. "And what about Tay's prosthetic ear? You've seen for yourself the technology they have. I saw firsthand the drugs used to keep people paralyzed, yet alive, while they were killed over twenty-four hours. I checked—that's not normal. Someone *crafted* that stuff specifically for its task. Why not be able to mess with brains, too? Besides, you said so yourself that you met a woman who seemed 'not herself' and that your team member, De'Leu, felt the same about another suspect."

"I know, I know!" Woods punched a fist into his other hand. "I've learned to accept many theories and I'm not opposed to this one, but I need proof. A few fleeting moments with someone who seems different is not enough to make me think Mags is not a killer."

Sean realized Woods was still upset about his team. In his eyes, Mags had been the culprit, even if she hadn't physically been there, simply because she was involved with the arson group.

Taking in a breath, he spoke. "I get it. Honestly, I'm pretty new to this line of thinking as well. I kept trying to rationalize what I saw with Angellica. I tried to explain away the difference with Violet. But when I heard from Mags...her words made it seem like...she's scared, you guys. And the idea of *each* of these women having alternate versions of themselves? It just makes more sense that they are being...reprogrammed, or whatever you want to call it, on purpose. These Triad women are capable of so many things we haven't ever thought about. Is it so farfetched to think they've figured this out, too?"

"It's not farfetched," Elaine chimed in. "I mean it is, but, it's just...holy crap, you know?"

Sean could tell by Woods' face that he still was debating it. Sean said, "I don't know how to provide you with proof. Angellica and Violet are both dead. The woman you saw and the one De'Leu met with are dead. The only thing I can think of is talking to the women from the bunker, maybe they know about this process? But you can't exactly stroll in there with me since we are trying to keep a low profile."

"Does it really matter if he believes this?" Elaine asked.

"Unfortunately, it does. We have to all be on the same page about what our end goal is." Sean turned towards Woods. "I know you wanted to interrogate Mags before you gave her over to the cops. What did you want to ask her about?"

"About the arson jobs, of course, and her connection to the Triads. But a different persona...?"

"If we catch her, are you going to turn her in?"

"Of course! She's killed people. She'll keep killing people."

"But what if it's not her?"

"Perhaps you just don't want it to *be* her," Woods sneered.

Sean's temper flared. "Maybe you don't care if she's a killer, you just want revenge for your team's deaths!"

"Guys," Elaine called out, standing up from the sofa. "This isn't going to get solved tonight. We are all tired and upset. I think we should sleep on it."

Sean thought about all the things he hadn't spoken about yet, including the district attorney's death he'd just learned about from Payne or about the website contact information he discovered. Elaine was right, though; he was exhausted and the throbbing in his head had taken an upswing. Plus, a small part of him questioned whether Woods was right. Did he so desperately want Mags to be innocent that he was willing to believe she was a different person? Or was it part of some elaborate scheme to get him to soften if he caught her? And yet, if Woods had seen this in a suspect once, too...it couldn't be a coincidence.

Right?

With a swirling mess of a mind, Sean couldn't think straight anymore.

"She's right," he said. "I don't think we can solve anything tonight." Glancing at the mess strewn all over and the notes on the wall, he added, "Woods, you're welcome to stay again."

"I think getting a hotel might be a better idea."

Sean looked up, now worried the Interpol agent was angry. But all he saw was weariness in his dark eyes.

"You shouldn't let anyone know yet that you're still alive," Sean cautioned.

"I'll check him in under my name," Elaine volunteered. "No one is looking for me. I'm just reporting on the story. They don't know I know anything more than that."

Sean nodded. "Thanks."

The two of them began to pack up their things. Sean shoved another bite of pizza into his mouth but chewed it without really noticing. His mind wandered instead. "How about we meet up in the morning, for breakfast?"

"Mind if we do it at my place?" Elaine asked, her gaze flitting around the small space. "I have a table and chairs."

Sean took the slight jab in stride. "Fine by me."

"Good. You can bring coffee. My maker's on the fritz." She shouldered her bag and flipped her hair to the opposite side. "Ready when you are."

"A few more moments," Woods replied, continuing to collect his things.

"You can leave the wall stuff here if you want," Sean offered. "Unless you think you're going to look everything over tonight."

Woods peered over at all the papers on the wall. "I suppose not. But I'd still like to have them with me." He turned his attention to Sean. "As much as I don't want to admit it, your words have a ring of truth to them. And…I did witness it. You're right. There are too many instances now of women seeming to not be themselves for this to be coincidence. Exactly what that means, I'm not sure. I'll have to reach out to some of my additional contacts to confirm."

"You want to bring others into this?"

"They are already in on it, although not everything that's occurred here the past few days. We keep contact to a minimum—for safety reasons. Six team members in total. Only two, though, could really help. The other four are more… resources…. rather than being of any real assistance to solve the case. Of the main two, one is stationed in London, the other in Madrid."

Sean paused in thought. "Have you talked to them since the explosion in the building?"

"No, why?"

"If it was someone on your team, an inside job, do *they* know about these other two agents?"

A look of fear crossed Woods' face. "Bloody hell…"

"I'd call them right now."

Woods nodded and stepped out of the apartment to get better reception.

"Poor guy," Elaine said. "He's holding together way better than I would."

"You're doing okay," Sean said lamely.

Elaine shook her head. "I barely even knew Gloria and I almost quit. This guy has lost several team members and people over the years to this stuff." She glanced at Sean. "You have, too." She frowned. "And now Charlotte's been taken? How can you not be jumping out of your skin?"

Sean gave out a weak laugh. "Who says I'm not? I just don't have anywhere to go once skinless. I don't know how to find her. Hell, I wouldn't have even known she was missing except Mags told me. Charlotte left me a voicemail saying she was working on an important case and would be gone for a while."

Sean thought about that. With Charlotte's situation changed from "helping" to "taken," eventually someone would notice her absence and report her missing. He wasn't sure about her personal life, but he knew she couldn't miss work too long without drawing suspicion. She loved her career and had worked hard for it. But if kidnapped, she couldn't notify anyone of her plans. Once that transpired, her coworkers would most likely report a problem. But what could they do? She'd just end up as another Missing Person's report. The Triads would make sure she was never found, alive or otherwise.

I have to find her, he thought. *But I have no idea where to start.*

Start with what you know, he reminded himself. *To find her, you need to understand more about these Triad women and the arsonists.*

At that moment, Woods reentered, his face drawn.

"Bad news?" Sean asked.

"Neither of my colleagues are answering their phones. As

for the other four, we usually just email, so I won't be able to do that until I can access my contact list...which was on the laptop destroyed in the fire."

"Not hearing from them doesn't have to mean anything bad, does it?" Elaine asked.

Woods ran a hand over his face. "If one didn't answer, perhaps, but both of them?"

"Try again later," Sean suggested. "Or tomorrow. You can't know if anything has happened to them until it's confirmed."

"This is a nightmare," Woods murmured, resuming the task of packing up his things.

Sean could relate. The worst of it was, he had this horrible gut feelings that things may get worse before they got better.

But how could things possibly get worse?

18

October 19th
1:00 a.m.

Squeeeeal.

Charlotte's eyelids flitted open at the sound.

Silence.

Must have been dreaming, she thought. Adjusting her pillow, she flipped to her other side, but then the manacle dug into her wrist, and she let out a hiss of pain. Rearranging herself once more, she accidentally knocked the cuff into the pipe next to her, and the reverberation vibrated through her arm.

Waiting until she drifted off again, she thought about the day. Between the recorded message and her talk with Mae, she'd hoped something else might have occurred, but even the promised food and water didn't arrive. So, she'd recited anatomy parts in her head, starting with the skull and moving down the body until she'd finally fallen asleep—somewhere around the hip bones.

I'll pick up there, she thought. *Iliac crest, Ilium, Sacroiliac joint...*

Slumber lulled her under until...

Squeeeeal.

Her eyelids popped open this time. She held her breath. Though dim, a little light filtered through the window on the wall, though whether moonlight or artificial, she wasn't sure. Either way, it shone through the glass just enough for her to see a silhouetted figure outside.

With quickened breaths, Charlotte readjusted her position to face the window. Her narrowed eyes couldn't reveal any more of the figure, so she merely waited. Every so often her gaze would sneak towards the door, to see if any outside guards had been alerted, but the door remained tightly closed.

Another squeal. Then, a muffled clank.

Slowly, ever so slowly, the frame of the window moved upwards. A crack, then a larger space, appeared. A cold draft drifted into the room. On it lingered the scent of sea water.

Near the ocean?

One last screech and the window lifted cleanly up to the halfway point. The figure, dressed in black, slid through.

Who could it be? Another Triad group? Suddenly a thought flickered through her mind, a thought filled with hope. *Maybe Mae has turned on them and is coming to get me out of here!*

Before she could determine if the intruder was friend or foe, Charlotte's fear shot into her throat. The front door began to open. A soft ray of light cut through the space from the opened entrance.

The intruder's head tilted towards the door's direction, and they sprinted forward, placing their back against the wall next to the door.

"I'm telling you," Charlotte heard someone whisper as they entered the room. "I heard something. Like metal scraping. I'm just gonna check her cuff."

Charlotte feigned sleep, keeping her eyelids the tiniest bit open. Footsteps could be heard coming closer, soft, but steady. Charlotte hoped the guard couldn't hear her heart pounding in her chest.

A slight movement around the manacle, then footsteps retreating.

"She's fine," the guard whispered.

"You were hearing things," said the other, further away.

"Maybe, but you know Mae would have a fit if—"

A noise, like a strangled word sounded.

"What the—" the guard furthest away said, this time without the whisper.

Charlotte opened her eyes to see the intruder had taken down the first guard. Now, they moved into the doorway. In a flurry of three or four quick movements, the other guard went down, being laid gently onto the floor.

Charlotte sat straight up, no longer feigning sleep. The intruder checked out into the hallway, whose light silhouetted them, so Charlotte still couldn't make them out. Finally, as if satisfied, the intruder pulled the two guards into the room and closed the door. A flick of a switch and light flooded the room. With quick steps, the intruder rushed over to Charlotte.

A glint of metal flashed in their palm.

Charlotte's heart thumped and her chest constricted.

They are here to kill me!

But the metallic object was moved over towards her own hand. In a few moments, the cuff came off. The intruder placed it on the blanket softly. Charlotte rubbed at her raw skin, wincing, but at the same time relishing the freedom from the shackle.

"Let's go," the intruder instructed, offering a hand to help Charlotte stand.

Charlotte recognized the Spanish accent.

"Carla?" she whispered in disbelief, her voice rough.

Carla pulled down the remainder of her black facial covering. "We must go now. Hurry."

A sense of relief melted through her chilled bones. Charlotte nodded, allowing the woman to assist her to her feet. After having been stuck on a cold floor for almost two days, her legs protested a bit, but the adrenaline rushing through her quickly countered the stiff feeling in her limbs. Still, she moved wobblier than she'd have liked. She wasn't quite sure how she'd be able to climb through the window.

Mid-thought, a voice rang out, muffled by the concrete walls.

"Stop!"

A louder noise followed--the door slamming open.

Charlotte turned her head at the same time as Carla to

view the newest addition to the room.

Mae stood in the doorway.

"No..." Charlotte muttered.

Carla made a motion and swept Charlotte behind her. "Head towards the window and go," she instructed.

Charlotte did as told, but the window sat too high for her to reach. Nothing caught her eye to boost her and besides, her legs had gotten more unstable, and she wondered how she'd get out at all. Pressing her back against the clammy wall, she watched as the two women approached each other.

"Carla," Mae said, rubbing a finger across her lower lip as if tasting the name. She carried a bag, which she dropped on the floor next to one of the unmoving guards' bodies.

Did she finally bring me more food? Charlotte wondered. Except the bag appeared to be a duffel bag, different from the translucent plastic bag which contained her meal earlier.

"You know me?" Carla replied. Charlotte noted the hint of surprise in her voice, though she hid it well.

"Oh, sure. I've heard all about you." Mae nodded at Carla's hands, which were positioned not in fists, but flat in the air with index and middle fingers pointed straight ahead like little snake heads. "You're famous for your pressure point attacks."

"They aren't all I know," Carla retorted, a threat hanging within the sentence.

"I'm sure. Still, I've always been curious to know who would be better."

"That must be difficult for you."

"Why's that?"

"Because since I don't know you, I won't think about you

for a second after I've beaten you. But you will have wasted time wondering about the outcome and then feeling the embarrasssment of failure."

At those words, Mae snarled and lunged.

Charlotte hardly had time to gasp before Carla struck. The blows were so quick—one seemed to hit Mae in the neck and the other near her armpit.

Mae retreated for a moment, her left arm now hanging limp by her side, but a smile smeared her face. A blade, which Charlotte hadn't even seen her pull out, sat in her good hand. A tinge of red smeared the edge.

Carla hadn't reacted at all, but Charlotte noticed a slice of red on her side where her shirt had shifted upwards.

"Point for each of us," Mae said, shaking her limp arm to no avail. "Question is, can you ragdoll me enough before you lose too much blood?"

They circled a bit again. Then slash, strike, slash. A sweep of the leg. A jump. An arc with sharp metal. A block. Two strikes. A stab.

The two women parted once more, this time with Mae leaning oddly to her right and Carla breathing heavily while blood dripped around her right shoe and onto the cement floor.

"You can't have her," Mae snapped. "I need her. She has to answer some ques—"

Strike. So fast. Charlotte barely registered the move. Straight into the middle of Mae's solar plexus. She wheezed a breath. Then one more strike with both hands to Mae's temples and her captor fell to the floor.

The only sound remaining was Carla's labored breathing. Carla stepped forward and leaned over the body.

"Do not kill her!" Charlotte heard herself cry out.

Carla paused. "Why not?" she asked, not looking away from Mae. "She wouldn't hesitate to kill you."

Charlotte's hands shook, but she peered over and saw Mags lying on the floor. She forced herself to think of her as Mae, a murderer who wouldn't hesitate to remove Charlotte from existence. And yet...she'd come here, in the middle of the night. Why? There were guards. There'd been no reason for Mae to come. She'd started to say she had questions. Had Charlotte gotten to her? Made her see that whatever plan she was following may not be legitimate?

But would any of her thoughts be enough reason for Carla to stand down? She didn't exactly have time to explain everything.

"Because..." Charlotte said, her chest tight. "Because I am telling you not to."

Carla finally looked over at Charlotte.

Charlotte continued. "This cannot be the way. Not anymore. Not for you or...or for the Triads." Charlotte's breath caught in her throat as she waited for a response. This was the first time she'd used her influence as the Messiah to restrict a Triad member.

"She may find you again."

Charlotte gave a weak nod. "Then she does so in our debt. That is not something to be taken lightly."

"She won't care about that."

"She might. And even if she does not, I will."

A few beats of silence passed. Carla then walked over to Charlotte as if she hadn't just killed two women and left a third unconscious on the floor.

Carla kneeled next to the wall. "Go."

Charlotte climbed onto her back and heaved herself through the frame. Sea air hit her face. With wide eyes, she searched the surroundings. Nothing looked familiar to her, but the briny scent wafted over her from the right, so she gathered that way must be east. Once out, she pressed herself against the side of the building until Carla had pulled herself through the window as well.

"This way."

Feeling more than a little exposed in a running outfit in the middle of the night, Charlotte followed quickly. Cold wind swirled around her, and her body became chilled quite fast. Faint clicks of her chattering teeth were the only sounds as they briskly walked to their new destination: a car about three blocks away. Every streetlight seemed a beacon lighting them up. Every alleyway or corner a new potential threat.

They arrived at the car without incident. Once inside, Carla turned on the engine, turned up the heat, and placed a puffy coat and blanket on Charlotte's lap. Dressing quickly, Charlotte rubbed her legs underneath the blanket.

"How are you?" Carla asked.

"Happy to see you," Charlotte replied. At those words, her eyes stung with tears of relief.

"Physically, though," Carla continued, turning away from the ocean towards inland. "Are you hurt? Hungry? Any drugs used?"

"Not hurt, except my wrist," she said, pulling out her hand. In the passing streetlights, she noted the black and blue marks and red chafing left behind from the cuff. "Definitely hungry, but mostly tired. And no, no drugs." She sniffled. "It was cold, though. And damp."

"Cold and hungry we can deal with." After another turn, Carla pulled into the parking lot of a motel. Nothing fancy, but it looked clean enough. Only about four other cars sat in the area.

They entered one of the rooms and Charlotte quickly stood near the radiating heat below the window. The closed curtains sported tiny gold diamonds amongst a charcoal-gray-checked background.

"Thank you," Charlotte finally managed, once the events of the evening fully sunk in.

"I'm only sorry I had to delay getting you out."

Charlotte raised an eyebrow.

"I've known your location since yesterday."

Memories of the past twenty-four hours rushed over her. "You mean you could have gotten me out at any point?"

"Technically, yes. But there have been...complications."

Warmth seeped through Charlotte's tired bones and the soft bed called to her as the adrenaline boost inside her slipped away. She wasn't sure if she could handle any more "complications" that night before setting her brain right again with some decent sleep.

"Can this wait until the morning?" Her eyes felt grainy and dry. Feeling returned to her fingertips and they hummed with heat. But the aches in her body suddenly hit her and she felt twenty years older.

Carla remained silent for several moments. "I suppose so."

"Good." With quick steps Charlotte closed the distance between herself and her goal, slid under the covers, and snuggled her face down into the pillow. She cared nothing for the grime covering her sweaty-and briny-covered clothes and skin. Compared to the cold, hard floor she'd been sleeping on, a feeling of heavenly bliss settled over her inside the clean, cozy surroundings.

"I'll wake you in the morning. We'll have to leave right away."

"Mmhmm..." Charlotte mumbled, already half asleep.

As she drifted off, she heard what sounded like Carla going through a checklist of the next day's events. The only thing that lodged its way into Charlotte's mind before slumber overtook her was the realization that all the plans only involved Carla and herself.

There was no mention of Isabella or Jordan.

19

October 19th
5:30 a.m.

Mae paced outside the warehouse, the adrenaline spiking inside her body making her mind rush through different ideas faster than she could interpret them. She'd spent most of the evening thinking about what Charlotte had asked her earlier that day: Why had the Coalition been added under Charlotte's direction as the Messiah?

Not only that, but someone had doctored that speech so it could be *proven* Charlotte wasn't the one who wrote it. How could she have been so foolish as to not see the contractions? That stupid perfect robot of a woman would never talk that way.

Because of these questions, Mae now found herself standing outside the warehouse in the middle of the night, debating whether or not she should talk with Charlotte further. Even with all her genius, she knew she must be too close to the situation to see it objectively.

Yet every fiber of her being found the idea of dealing with Charlotte repulsive. How could she even *think* about talking to a fake Messiah? Charlotte represented the most corrupt version of a Triad woman—someone willing to manipulate and lie to seek power. How could Mae believe anything she would say? It was Charlotte's job to spin truths to get anyone on her side.

The nagging doubts plagued Mae throughout her time on the job that night—to set fire to another third's location. She hadn't enjoyed the act of arson, nor the murder of the treacherous woman who believed in Charlotte's validity, like she usually did.

What's wrong with me? she thought as she had driven towards her hotel. *Why am I letting these stupid thoughts get to me?*

But instead of heading to the safety of her hotel and the pleasure in the arms of Patrick, she found herself driving to the warehouse. And now, here she stood in front of the doors, pacing.

Not only that, but she'd also brought an duffel bag with her, packed with items in case she chose to help Charlotte escape.

This is stupid, she thought. *I should just leave. I trust the true Messiah. I don't need to believe in Charlotte's lies.*

Even if she *did* end up believing Charlotte, what could she do about it? If she released the prisoner, she'd only be hunted down, and Charlotte with her. Why on Earth had she thought Charlotte's release could be an option?

I'm not thinking straight. Sleep on it. Come back in the morning.

Instead, she opened the doors to the warehouse and headed inside.

As she moved down the stairs towards the basement, she heard a thump, then another, with a muffled yell coming from the hallway.

What the...?

Keeping quiet, she peered through the doorway and down the hall. The body of one of the guards lay on the ground, while the other's feet could only be seen through the door to the room where Charlotte was being kept. Mae yanked her head backwards and waited as she heard the sounds of the bodies being dragged inside. After a few more moments, she crept down the hallway. Pressing her ear against the door, she couldn't hear anything, but she did see a sliver of light peeking from underneath the entrance.

Taking a deep breath, Mae grasped the knife in her pocket before shoving the door open.

"Stop!" she cried out at the intruder and Charlotte who were both headed towards the open window.

The intruder turned around and faced Mae.

Oh my God, it's Carla. A sense of unreality washed over Mae. She'd heard so much about this third from South America. She'd learned about Carla's way of fighting, her moves, her perspectives on the world. A sense of fear mingled with the thrill of excitement at facing off with what she thought of as her counterpart.

Gripping the knife in her hand, Mae moved forward...

Mags' eyelids squeezed shut, not wanting to open. She didn't want to face this terrifying woman. But then reality seeped in. Mags was no longer standing. She wasn't Mae anymore, but still lay on the cold floor where Mae had fallen, her body aching, especially in her head and left arm.

Apparently, we fought, she thought. *And Mae lost.*

"Unghhh..." she managed before sitting up. The room swayed. Once it settled into solidity, she glanced around. Two bodies lay near the door to her left; the open window and remaining shackle on the ground near some pipes to her right. The sky outside still appeared dark, although she felt like the faintest traces of light could be seen in the furthest sky.

Quickly assessing the situation, she realized she was nowhere near the hotel and so couldn't send an email to Sean to let him know that Charlotte had been taken or perhaps rescued by a woman named Carla.

Not that it mattered anyway. Mags could already feel a pang of pain forming in her head.

Already? Her time remaining as Mags was getting shorter and shorter. She knew at some point she wouldn't wake up as herself again.

Checking Mae's pockets, Mags found a phone, revealing the time as once again early morning. Did she have time to find a computer?

Mags stared at the phone. *Wait a minute...* The screen

glowed. Luck appeared to be on her side because the phone was unlocked. *I can make a phone call,* she thought, hope flaring in her chest.

But do I risk it?

Mags knew her counterpoint's situation had begun to deteriorate. With her doubts, Mae may not last much longer within the Triads. Not if someone found out.

Throwing caution to the wind, Mags decided anonymity couldn't be a factor anymore. This call may be her only hope...

20

October 19ᵗʰ
8:00 a.m.

Sean finished pulling on his jacket as he hurried to get ready and make his appointment with Woods and Elaine at her place. He couldn't believe how much he'd slept, including through his alarm. After everyone had cleared out the previous night, he thought for sure he wouldn't be able to sleep at all as he mulled over what their plan might be for the following day. But, surprisingly enough, as soon as he'd sat down on his couch, put on some action movie, and drank Payne's beer, he'd conked out.

Now he'd only have the car ride over to think about how they would all proceed. He'd have to work through things quickly, but he believed he had an idea of what they could each do. And none of the plan centered around whether Woods or Elaine believed him about Mags. Though...eventually they'd have to.

Just before he left, he grabbed a slice of leftover pizza from the fridge, shoved half of it into his mouth, and opened his apartment door. Juggling the remaining pizza in one hand and his keys in the other, he heard the cellphone in his pocket beep now that he'd gotten a little reception.

Hope nothing else came up. Maybe Elaine has to cancel? Or there's news about Woods' people or more about which one of his team wasn't in the fire?

Removing his keys after locking the door, he pulled the phone out and listened to the message. An automated voice told him the voicemail had been forwarded through his work line.

Sean frowned. It was pretty rare for any calls to come for him on weekends to the precinct and be sent to his cell phone. Not unheard of, but unusual.

Well, I doubt it's from Woods or Elaine then. They could just call my cell directly.

Moving down the stairs, he listened to the message. The voice on the other end stopped him dead between floors.

"Hey Sean, it's Mags. Couldn't email you. No longer at the hotel. Using Mae's phone but I didn't remember your cell number. Thought through work would be best."

Her words were breathy and quick, as if Mags were terrified of being caught...or possibly in pain?

"Okay," she continued. *"Update. Charlotte's been taken.*

Or rescued. Not sure which. Mae fought back to keep her in the warehouse but based on me waking up face down on the concrete floor, I'm pretty sure she lost. Ouch!"

A pause.

"Not a lot of time left. This time I'm here shorter. Don't know if I'll come back." Sean could hear the terror in her voice. *"What you need to know is this: Mae is having doubts. Don't know how badly, but she wanted to talk to C, get answers to her questions about what's really going on with the arson group. OUCH! SHIT! Stupid head, not yet! So anyway, she may be able to turn against who she works for. That's all I can give you. I hope it's enough....Oh yeah! The kidnapper or rescuer or whoever who took C is named Carl—OW!"*

The message ended abruptly.

Sean couldn't move. He'd completely forgotten he wanted to check his work email in case Mags sent another message. He counted himself thoroughly lucky that she'd left a message on his phone instead. The information would have been lost otherwise, or at least not received until he returned to work on Monday.

Realization of what her words meant sunk in. Mags was in trouble, real trouble, of disappearing forever. Charlotte had either been saved from Mae or kidnapped by someone else—someone named Carl? And Mae herself was having doubts. If found, could she help them stop the other Triads? Or find Charlotte?

On top of all that, though, was that Mags hadn't tried to hide herself anymore. She'd called him from a cellphone. He could track that number from work. He could find Mae's location.

They had a lead.

Sean's brain jumpstarted at that thought and his body followed suit. Leaping down the rest of the stairs, he tore through the lobby and out of the building to his car. Once in, he raced down the street, following the directions spewing from his GPS to bring him to Elaine's.

Arriving about ten minutes later, he found her apartment number on the intercom, and was buzzed up. Elaine let him in after he knocked on the door.

"Hey guys," he said, waltzing into the space. Elaine's two-bedroom apartment looked like a mansion compared to his studio. With wide windows, green curtains, and plants spread all over, it felt a little like a greenhouse. Scents of flowering vines and moist earth hit him and brought him into memories of helping his mom in their garden back in Philly.

"I told you he'd forget," Elaine said to Woods, a smug look on her face.

Sean frowned. "Forget what?"

"The coffee."

Sean cringed. "Oh, crap, yeah it completely slipped my mind. Sorry. I woke up late and—"

"Don't worry. I was up early so I grabbed some." Condescension covered the words.

Sean wanted to snap a retort, but he figured there wouldn't be a point. They'd all ended their meetup on an argument last night and he didn't want to start another one.

Remembering what had transpired, Sean glanced over at Woods, trying to determine if he still held any residual anger, but the British man gave away nothing on his face.

Elaine passed Sean a cup of coffee and returned to the kitchen table, at which Woods already sat, his coffee in hand, but not being drunk.

"Let's get started," Elaine said, once again taking charge. "I was just chatting with Inspector Woods here about what he learned." Her face fell. "It's not good news."

"What now?" Sean asked, feeling the little amount of hope he had at a possible lead vanish like a candle blowing out.

"I heard about those two contacts I called last night, the ones in Madrid and London," Woods said, his voice hollow. "Both dead."

Shock coursed through Sean. "Dead?"

"Yes. Both fires. One at home, one at work."

Two more deaths, these international, in different countries. Were there no limits to what these women could accomplish? Or any care about how many people they killed?

"When?"

"Almost the same time as the fire in the building my team and I met in." Woods shook his head and let out a huge sigh. "I bloody hate to admit it, but it had to be Leeds who coordinated the effort. Her body wasn't found in the explosion."

"Yeah," Elaine said. "I asked around this morning to get IDs on the bodies. I mean, your crew," she said quickly.

"Leeds...?" Sean asked. "Was there any indication that she would double cross your team?"

Woods shook his head. "She was our most recent member. Came from the Australian Federal Police. She'd only been with us for about four months."

"I thought you said you vetted everyone?" Elaine asked.

"I did." Woods' words came out sharp. "I'm not a plonker. I even spoke to her commanding officer. High recommendations. Nothing amiss."

Sean thought about how Angellica had seamlessly been a part of society, how Violet's alternate persona, Veronica, ran an animal shelter. How the bunker had been completely self-sufficient, except for stolen electricity and water. The coordination, connections, even the resources of these women stretched far beyond synchronized killings. They prided themselves on blending in, creating plausible scenarios to keep their covers intact. And they'd been doing it for centuries. With current technology, a lot of their covers could be more easily procured, if they had the computer knowhow.

Sean thought about Mags. That woman could hack into any processor she wanted. Establishing a fake phone number to call for a "reference" would be fairly simple for this group.

"Did you only speak to one person about Leeds?" Sean asked slowly. "And did Leeds provide the contact number?"

"Well of course, but..." Woods trailed off. "She set me up, didn't she? Brilliant. Just bloody brilliant. I got my entire team killed!" A flick of his hand accidentally knocked over the coffee cup in front of him, spilling the drink across the table.

"Eep!" Elaine cried out, standing quickly. She rushed into the kitchen and returned with a roll of paper towels, mopping the spill efficiently. "No problem," she said. "No damage done."

"I apologize," Woods said, having pushed his chair away from the table while Elaine cleaned. "I got us all into this whole mess."

"No more than any of the rest of us," Sean said. "They've fooled a lot of us. Hell, I almost married one of them."

Woods cracked a tiny smile out of the side of his mouth, then his face fell. "It's still my fault."

"No," Sean said forcefully. A thread of memory floated through his mind from one of his mandatory therapy sessions he recently underwent with Carla. "You're not the first person to be the focus of a killer. But whatever you did, you aren't responsible for their actions. They are."

Woods didn't reply, but Sean saw him exhale a little more forcefully. "Easy to say…"

"I know. But it's the truth. Otherwise we'll each blame ourselves every time something bad happens."

Quiet descended, except for the gentle wiping of the paper towels.

"Well, I think it's about time we figured out a plan," Elaine said, cutting across the silence. She chucked the sloppy mess of paper into a wastebasket behind her. "I have some ideas—"

"Wait," Woods interrupted. "We need to talk about Mags before moving forward. Sean's right. We can't be in the same group if we are not on the same page."

Sean swallowed nervously. "I take it you thought about it?"

"Couldn't stop. Especially after hearing about what happened to the rest of my group. Truth is, it's a lot more believable to think that Leeds wasn't really herself when she set the fire."

"You don't know for sure if Mags is a different person, though," Elaine said. "I mean, we don't know if she's a Triad agent that was...reprogrammed or whatever...or just joined the group, right?"

Woods said, "True. But based on what Trann believes... Not only that, but I know what I saw with my own murder suspect. I know what I was told on the phone from my anonymous tip. And De'Leu felt the same way. On top of that, you were right last night, Trann. These Triads...they can perform extraordinary feats, both with technology and medicine. They've pushed past many limits we currently know." He crossed his arms. "I will believe that Mags may be an alternate persona. However, if we find her, I'll need to know for sure. There has to be some proof."

Tense energy surged away from Sean's body. "And you, Elaine?"

She shrugged. "In for a penny, in for a pound. But I agree with Inspector Woods. I'm first and foremost a journalist. I'll have to see proof to believe it. For right now, between you both, there's enough for me to follow up on the theory and see where it goes."

"Great. That's great. Because..." Sean took a deep breath. "I heard from Mags this morning. She left me a message on my phone. We may be able to trace the call."

Woods frowned. "I thought she planned to keep her whereabouts secret?"

"It seems as if things have gotten more complicated for her, or at least for her counterpart." Sean dialed up the message on his phone and played it for them all on speakerphone.

"She sounds really scared," Elaine said.

"And as though she's putting herself in peril by contacting

you," Woods added.

"It could be an act," Sean suggested, testing the waters.

"It could be," Woods replied, "but exposing her own location, giving us information about the group and Charlotte's predicament...those seem like odd things for someone to do if they weren't being sincere."

"Unless it's a trap," Elaine said. "She could be luring us so they can get us all."

Sean shook his head. "I don't think so. If that were the case, she could have told me in the email where they'd taken Charlotte and set a trap there."

Woods suggested, "Maybe she thought you wouldn't believe she wasn't a killer? I mean, everyone is after her."

"Except there would have been no reason to reach out to me at all. No need to expose herself. No, no one apart from Elaine knew I was even still looking into the Triads."

"Leeds knew I was bringing you into the group," Woods added. "She could have told Mags and set all this up." Woods spoke again before Sean could. "But like you said, that doesn't make any sense. It's too elaborate. If they thought you were looking into Triad-related information, Mags knows where you live. You could have been killed in a fire at any point in time."

Sean cleared his throat. "There's another reason to go along with that thought process. You remember when my partner, Payne, showed up last night? Well, he had some news. He's not fully on duty yet, but he'd been listening in on his police scanner, probably feeling helpless while the search goes on for Mags. Anyway, he told me the district attorney assigned to the Triad trial was killed two nights ago."

Elaine perked up. "Jordan Parker? I interviewed her after the trial."

Sean nodded. "Stabbed three times, but afterwards, her apartment was set on fire. And an eyewitness says someone fitting Mags' description fled the scene. So, I agree with you, Woods. If Mags wanted me dead, all she'd have to do was show up and kill me. I think this 'Mae' persona doesn't think I'm a threat, so I haven't been targeted."

"A final reason is that Mags said in her message Mae may turn. There's no reason to say that unless she wanted you to talk to Mae first."

"Exactly, Elaine."

The three of them sat in silence for a few moments, the only sound the humming of Elaine's nearby space heater. Sean didn't know what the other two mulled over during the quiet, but so much tension had melted from his body he suddenly felt twenty pounds lighter. They actually believed him about the possibility of Mags' innocence. Even though he still had a hard time considering the concept himself, working through the explanations with them helped give the idea more credibility.

"So then, what's the plan?" Elaine finally asked. "All my ideas are pretty much shot to crap now."

"Well, I have a few thoughts, but it'll mean splitting up for the day," Sean answered.

"One of them has to be tracing the call," Woods inserted. "We need to find the location of that cell number as soon as possible."

"Of course, but we don't have to sit around all day waiting

for the results. Besides, it's Saturday. I may not hear anything until the work week, though I'll try to insist it's a priority. It may be tough, though, without giving a reason for the rush."

Woods asked, "So what do you have in mind in the meantime?"

Sean tapped on his phone, pulling up some notes he made from work the previous day.

"All right. Since we ended things a little early last night, there are a few things I didn't get to talk about. The first: I looked up the contact info on those websites you provided, Elaine."

"Any luck?" she asked.

"Yeah."

"What websites?" Woods asked.

"The ones that posted possible Triad agents and the one that had the 'Messiah' audio clip," Elaine replied. She scowled. "I told you about them last night."

"Apologies. There was a lot of information last night," Woods said, his tone a bit brisk.

"I'm sure it won't be the last time one of us doesn't re-member something," Sean said, smoothing things over. He couldn't believe how quickly this group could get upset. He missed working with Wilt and Tay and Mags and Charlotte and...

Sean shook away those thoughts. They were a fantasy. Things could never be way again. "Anyway, I got info on both websites. The first one, with the list of agents, comes from Springfield, Pennsylvania. That's just west of Philly. The second is just outside Rochester in New York. Couldn't get a verified name for the first one, it's under a Roswall Corp—probably some alternate spelling nod to Roswell plus Area 51—but the second one is under someone named..." Sean could hear the shuffling of papers in the background. "Named Zack Union. I figured we could try to contact each of them, ask them questions about their websites? In person would be best—less chance to dodge our attempts."

"How far away are they?"

"Each place is pretty much the same distance, just different directions. About five and a half, maybe six hours with traffic."

"I want to talk to the Zack guy," Elaine said immediately. "I want to know more about those audio clips, especially since we know it's Charlotte's voice. If we can track down where he got them, maybe it'll help to find her?"

"Maybe, but remember, she recently left wherever Mae was holding her last night."

Elaine pouted.

"I had something different in mind for you anyway," Sean said.

"What's that?"

"To go and speak with the women in the bunker. It won't seem as strange for you to be interviewing them. Woods obviously can't go—we still have to keep his location a secret—and I probably shouldn't go because I don't need to draw any suspicion to myself that I'm still looking into anything Triad related."

Woods asked, "Then you'd like me to visit this Mister Union?"

Sean nodded. "That leaves me checking out the Roswall

location. I know Philly pretty well anyway, and this place is pretty close to town, so I can always say I went home for a visit."

The three of them discussed the plan further and after an hour or so of figuring out exactly what questions they wanted to ask from their prospective interviewees, they decided to part ways.

As they gathered their stuff to leave, Elaine's phone pinged.

"Oh God," she said.

"What?" Sean asked, wondering how there could be anything worse than what had already occurred.

"I programmed my phone to alert me if there were any more posts from the website that had the audio clip. Something new just came out." She opened the website and they all listened to the forty-second sample.

"Hey all, it's me, Zack Attack. You know you've been waiting for me, and I won't disappoint. Here it is, further proof that the Triads are out there, they have a leader, and they don't have any problem torching those that get in their way! Listen up!"

A few seconds of silence passed and then, in Charlotte's voice: *"I understand that this path isn't easy for many of you to hear. Those who resist will meet with the same fate as any who disobey my orders. You have heard of the fires. You have heard of the Coalition. They are under my rule to dispose of any Triad members who don't follow my orders."*

Zack's voice returned. *"Stay tuned, followers, to hear more!"*

Elaine closed the site. "Is it...?"

"Yeah. It's Charlotte." Sean frowned. He tried to focus on what she'd said, but something else bothered him. The words themselves? "But...something isn't quite right..."

"What?"

"I don't know. But...she sounds...wrong. Not entirely like herself."

Woods asked, "Like her voice had been doctored?"

"No. Just...not right." He tapped on her phone. "Send me the link. I'll listen to it while I'm driving. Maybe I can figure it out."

Elaine did so. "Sounds like the arsonists have a name."

Woods ground his jaw. "The Coalition. And your girlfriend is in charge of them," he said to Sean.

Sean's jaw tightened. "That can't be right. Charlotte would never..."

"Mags did," Elaine said softly.

"As did my team member, Leeds," Woods added.

Sean's thoughts spun. He knew what they were implying. That Charlotte was an alternate persona as well. "I know what you're thinking. It's just...I think it's different for Charlotte. Not just because of how I feel about her, but because of the facts. She was kidnapped by Truth six months ago and *told* she was their Messiah. She was almost killed for that same reason. If she were a covert fake person, why put her in that position? And wouldn't she have already known if she secretly worked for them?"

Elaine flipped her hair. "That's a good point."

"But she just confessed to using the Coalition to track down other non-cooperative Triad members," Woods said.

"I know." Sean shrugged into his jacket. "And I know how bad this looks. But I'm telling you," he said, thinking once again about her words, "something isn't right."

21

October 19th
10:00 a.m.

Oni rolled her eyes. "I'm turning thirty-five tomorrow. When are you going to stop treating me like a child?"

"When you stop pretending you aren't in danger!" The woman on the phone *tsked* at her daughter. "You are not thinking things through. I saw what you posted on the internet. Your website is *not* the reason I came forwards three years ago to tell you about the Triads. All you've done is put a target on your own head!"

Oni shifted her purse from one shoulder to the other. Slightly higher than normal temperatures and the shining sun were making her sweat more than she'd like. But soon she'd be once again in her craptacular apartment where she spent most of her time obsessing over her Triad website.

She had to admit, her mother was right. Ever since she'd gotten the anonymous phone call three years ago, telling her to investigate an odd criminal proceeding, she'd been intrigued. Proud of her Master's degree in psychology, Oni never pursued her career further than social work—even though it could be demanding and difficult—because that phone call changed everything. A whole new world opened up to her, one where even the most mundane mother-of-three with normal financial and emotional difficulties between herself and her girls could turn into a brainwashed, fake persona who actually killed people once a month!

"I'm being careful," Oni replied, wiping a dash of sheen from her dark forehead. She was glad she kept her hair short and natural. She couldn't imagine carrying the weight of the braids she wore a few years ago.

"No, you're not. In your latest post you mentioned Mags Stinton—the woman from Boston who killed a police detective. She's big game, sweetie. Those in her circle will be looking for references to her. They'll track you down."

Oni fought the urge to roll her eyes again. "*Everyone* is talking about her. All I did was connect the dots to the Triads."

"Everyone is talking about her as a murderer, NOT a Triad agent!"

She hefted her bag once more, wishing she hauled less, but knowing she would never actually take the time to empty the cumbersome purse. "Well, it's your own fault. You taught me what patterns to look for, what inconsistencies to narrow in on.

I can't help it if it's plain as day to me who she really is. And this whole Triad nonsense has been kept under wraps for long enough. It's time they were exposed."

Oni could feel the anger seeping through the phone even though her mother didn't say a word. Suddenly, her toe caught on a sidewalk crack, and she went down, hitting the ground, hard.

"Damnit!" she said. Her hand had twisted under the weight of the fall and pain shot through her wrist.

"You okay?"

Oni could hear the question coming from her phone, which had fallen to the ground. She picked it up and cursed again. The screen had a huge scratch across it.

"I'm fine," she snapped into the phone, picking up her purse from the ground. A new pain sizzled in her knee, and she checked it. Below the hemline of her skirt sat an ugly scrape, bleeding slightly. "I fell," she blurted. "Look, I gotta go. I'm almost home."

"Wait, sweetie, I'm sorry. But you have to—"

Oni hung up. She'd heard the lecture dozens of times over the past few years, ever since she'd pressed the woman, who'd wanted to stay anonymous, into confessing the truth about their relationship: she was Oni's birth mother.

That bit of news had been more of a shock than the idea of Triads. For one, she hadn't known she was adopted. And two, her newfound mother had told Oni about being a Triad member, getting pregnant, and the running away until she'd given birth. She'd had twins and split them up, hoping they'd have better success on their own than together. The third bombshell, then, included a long-lost sibling out in the world as well.

Some days Oni wished she'd never heard from her birth mother and other days she couldn't imagine continuing to live in the dark now that she knew the truth about the Triads. She'd dedicated most of her life the past three years to discovering agents or possible members. When the Triad trial hit in Boston six months ago, her readership skyrocketed. She actually started making money off her blogs and commentaries. But she'd always been very careful to remain unknown. She couldn't see any way for a Triad member to track her down. Her mother was just being overcautious, as usual.

On her way up the stairs to the door of her apartment building, Oni froze. She wasn't sure why, but something didn't feel right. If there was anything she'd learned from her birth mother, it was to be aware of her surroundings.

Oni bent over as if tying her shoe and surveyed the area peripherally.

There. Halfway down the block. A woman standing, leaning against her car. She'd been staring at Oni and now looked away, gazing up at the apartment building in front of her.

Under normal circumstances, the woman merely appeared as if she was waiting for a friend to exit the building and had cursorily glanced in Oni's direction. Maybe she saw Oni fall and watched to make sure she was all right. Maybe her cute green skirt had caught the woman's admiring eye.

But Oni knew differently. She'd had a stalker once—the incident was actually why she'd gotten into psychology in the first place. A young man she knew from high school. The way he'd stared at her across the cafeteria was the same way this woman peered over at her now. Even though the glance had been brief, Oni recognized the identical look.

Greedy and possessive.

Like hunting a target.

Oni stood, thinking fast. *Can't go inside—I'll be trapped. Public place is safer. Then call my mother.* She fumbled around in her purse, pretending to search for something.

"Damn!" she said, loudly enough so the woman could hear her. She pulled out her phone and placed a fake phone call. *Gotta set this up. Give a name of a place. Say where I am now. Can't be taken if someone knows where I am and where I'm going.*

"Hey Marcia," she said, choosing the name of a cousin of hers. She walked straight past the woman waiting outside the car. It was risky, but she needed to prove she didn't suspect any-thing. "I just got home, but realized I left my notes at your apartment. I'm on my way. Should be there in about twenty minutes. The bus picks up right at the end of my street." Once out of earshot, Oni stepped up her pace, turned the corner, and ducked inside the nearest coffee shop. She waited with bated breath until she saw the bus come and go, hoping the woman would believe she was on it.

Sure enough. Moments later, a car, with the woman in the driver's seat, followed behind the bus.

Oni moved to the rear of the café and pulled out her phone. "Mom?" she said after dialing. "I'm in trouble. What do I do?"

22

October 19th
10:30 a.m.

"Charlotte, wake up."

The urgent words wafted through the sleepy haze over Charlotte, and she reluctantly opened her eyes. For several moments she had to place both the face looming over her and the location of her current whereabouts, a recent trend she'd begun to despise.

I am with Carla in a hotel room. I am no longer in the warehouse. I am safe.

"We need to leave, now." Dark eyes filled with determination and a bit of fear bore into her own.

"All right, okay," Charlotte muttered, the words thick in

her mouth. She'd been dreaming, a wonderful dream about rolling around on white, fluffy clouds which melted into a warm milk bath. Women hovered around her, just out of reach, while she pulled their puppet strings. Every time they reached out to take something in the room, she pulled them away. Slowly, they stopped reaching, and their angry faces turned joyful.

"What is going on?" Charlotte asked, clearing away the lingering images from her dream and focusing on her current predicament.

"I'll tell you once we are on our way." Carla threw a backpack on the bed next to Charlotte. The bag bounced beside her, causing her body to move. It triggered an uncomfortableness in her bladder, causing her to realize she really needed to use the bathroom.

"Okay. Let me get my head together. Where is the restroom?"

"No time. You can go once we are on the road."

Charlotte's abdomen twisted at the thought of holding anything in. "I really have to go."

Carla let out a sharp exhale. "Fine. But quickly. Please." She took Charlotte's arm and pulled her out of the bed, guiding her towards the restroom door. "Go. Hurry!"

Charlotte stumbled into the space, still half awake. As she pulled down the sweatpants given to her by Mae to sit, she realized how gross her state of being had become. Between stiff, caked-on, creased clothing and body odor, she felt absolutely disgusting.

Once relieved, she washed her hands, splashed some cold

water on her face, and rinsed out her mouth. When she got to the door, she could only open it a crack before—

"LOCK THE DOOR!" Carla ordered, closing the door in her face.

Suddenly, Charlotte felt wide awake as adrenaline coursed through her. She could hear voices outside the bathroom. From what she could determine, there were two of them: both female.

"She is the true Messiah. You know this." Carla's words held desperation in them, but Charlotte could also hear a hint of threat.

Muffled voices replied.

"You will not use her any longer." A strangled yelp, then a thump.

Charlotte retreated from the door, feeling completely helpless. With quick glances, she once again looked around herself for a weapon, just like in the warehouse, but nothing came into view. All she could do was hope Carla could defeat them. And this time, she didn't care if they died. Terror overtook her and her breathing became ragged in her chest. More noises, like an ensuing fight, before silence.

A quiet knock. "It's all right. It's me."

A shaky breath struggled from her lungs and Charlotte rushed to the door to unlock it. She flung it open and stumbled out, clinging to Carla for support. Two bodies lay on the floor, but if they were alive or not, Charlotte couldn't tell through her blurred eyes.

"Let's go," Carla said, gently leading Charlotte to the door. With her free hand, Carla swooped up the backpack, grabbed an extra coat from the back of a chair, and they left.

"We will be taking that car," she said, pointing to a black four-door sedan a few doors down. Carla clicked open the locks. "Wait there. I will join you soon."

Charlotte headed towards the car and got into the passenger side, her body shaking. She recognized the signs of an anxiety attack and did her best to breathe slowly and concentrate on grounding herself. It worked, a bit, but the lightheaded feeling hadn't quite dissipated by the time Carla got into the driver's seat.

"I called 911 to request an ambulance and left the phone off the hook so they could trace the call."

"They are not dead?" Charlotte asked, her teeth chattering. The short walk to the car had chilled her still damp face.

Carla swallowed and her jaw tightened. "I know you... frown...on killing. They will live but will be out of commission for several days. Their insides are...unhappy."

Charlotte smiled at Carla's use of a translated word. Her English was very good, but occasionally, she said something that seemed a little off.

"Who were they?" Charlotte asked, her head still spinning. She moved her hands in front of the heater vent when Carla turned it up.

"If I had to guess?" Carla said, pulling out of the parking lot. "I would assume Coalition members."

"Already?" The rapidity of their movements astounded her. "How did they find us? And so fast!"

Carla didn't speak at first.

"Carla?" Charlotte turned her head to look at the woman. Though her stare stretched to the road in front of them, her knuckles paled because of their tight grip.

"I'm not sure."

Charlotte heard the words, but for some reason she didn't believe them. She wasn't certain if Carla believed them.

"You are not sure?" Charlotte pressed.

Carla let out a sigh and her shoulders dropped. "There are...factors involved which I didn't consider. Until now. But these factors...I have a difficult time believing they could be true."

"Perhaps I could help?"

Carla shook her head. "Before we do that, I need to talk with you first. I need to know everything about your kidnapping. Oh, and there is some food in the backpack. You should eat something while we talk."

Charlotte pulled the knapsack from the backseat and combed through its contents until she found a brown paper bag with the food. "What would you like to know?"

"You went for a run with Isabella two mornings ago, correct?"

Has it really only been two days? Charlotte shook away the thought of incredulity. "Yes," she answered.

"*You* wanted to go for a run?"

Choosing a protein bar and a V8, she replied, "Yes. Well, Isabella suggested it. She had just returned from obtaining supplies. She said we had some down time and probably would not get much more after that. It sounded wonderful to me."

"Did she choose the route?"

Charlotte struggled to remember. She was distracted for a few moments as an ambulance went flying by, sirens blazing. She knew it must be headed towards the hotel. "Neither of us chose it. We just sort of...followed a path around the campground."

"And when you returned, the RV was already ablaze?"

Charlotte nodded, then took a swig from her drink. The tomato-y flavor hit her tastebuds hard, causing her to wince for a moment. "Raging. People had already collected around it to watch."

"No chance the Book survived?"

Charlotte remembered the pain on Isabella's face as she realized the Book had still been inside the vehicle.

"Not that I could think of. Half the camper was already melted."

"Then what happened?"

"I pulled Isabella away and called you. You told us to meet you at the restaurant and we headed there."

"No contact with Jordan?"

A big bite out of the protein bar kept her quiet for a few moments before she answered. "No. I planned to, but you said you were going to call her."

"That's right. Yes, I did. Let her know what was going on. Then I went to meet you at the restaurant, but you weren't there." Carla pulled onto the freeway.

"Did Jordan come with you?"

"No. I told her to stay put. I haven't heard from her since, though. That's what concerns me."

"It has only been about a day and a half."

"She would have answered the phone. Unless..." Carla swerved around the semi next to her.

"Unless what?" Charlotte's head had finally cleared, but now her stomach growled, hungry for more. She'd barely eaten anything in the past couple of days and her body was protesting the mere morsels she currently gave it. Another big bite.

"Unless she's involved."

The sentence hung in the air as Carla exited the freeway.

"Involved?" Charlotte asked, mid-chew. She couldn't imagine how that could be possible. She'd barely seen Jordan since Charlotte had decided to jump on board with the whole "Messiah" concept. The only time they'd been in contact was when Jordan gave the news that she believed Mags worked for the Triads. Why would she have told them that if she was involved with them?

Carla turned onto a side street. "She's the only one who knew where the RV was. She's the last of us to come into the Triad world. And she knew our moves, our aliases, everything."

"You really believe she could be helping them?"

"I'm saying that the only way the Coalition members could locate me was if someone knew my false names. They would have been able to check nearby hotels to find us."

"And Jordan would have known those aliases?"

Carla nodded as she took one more turn. "It's time for me to give Jordan a visit." The darkness in her voice came through loud and clear.

Charlotte took another drink, then, hoping to calm Carla down she said, "You don't know it is her."

"She's the only one left."

Charlotte remained silent as they drove down the block. She couldn't navigate this world anymore. How could anyone trust anyone? Half the time they weren't even their real selves. And now there was video out there of her claiming responsibility for the Coalition and the fires. How would she ever have her life back? And how could she ever know who to believe?

Glancing over at Carla, an unease rolled through her. Did this mistrust extend to her, too?

You cannot go down this road. There is no way to know anything unless you have all the facts, which you may never have. All you can do is stick with people who seem to have your best interests in mind. Carla appears to be one of those people.

Carla parked the car on the street. "Wait here. I'll return shortly."

"What are you going to do?" She tossed the empty protein bar wrapper back into the paper bag.

Carla paused. "If she is responsible for your capture, for your treatment, for the destruction of the Book, for the deaths of multiple Triad members..." She trailed off.

Charlotte rubbed her forehead between her eyebrows. "I do not know what to do here. How can we possibly deal with this? How can we bring her to justice? Do we even have any proof? Any witnesses? It is not as if *you* could testify. You have killed people as well."

Carla simply waited.

"I suppose you have gone through all these questions yourself already."

Carla rubbed her hands together, staring down at them.

"Isabella and I were very thorough in our process before we ever terminated a Triad member."

"But ultimately you decided to kill them." It was a statement more than a question.

"These women...I was, *am,* one of them. I was flawed. My desire for retribution and revenge pushed me into a vigilante state of being. It's partially how I was recruited in the first place. But when they took my *querida,* my love..." Carla closed her eyes briefly, twirling the ring on her left hand. "They cared more that I stayed obedient than for the wellbeing of an innocent. We offer this same opportunity to the thirds, to give up their duty and stop killing."

"Isabella said they never took the deal. That they refused to turn themselves in."

"Yes. Isabella negotiated with them. If they weren't compliant, either she or I would return to finish the task, to make sure they didn't hurt anyone ever again."

Charlotte thought about that. "But not Jordan?"

"Not Jordan...what?"

"She did not kill any non-compliant thirds?"

Carla shook her head. "Jordan never had any interest in killing."

"Yet...you think she has been masterminding this whole plot with the Coalition, killing dozens of women, and kidnapping?"

Carla chewed on her lower lip. "The evidence points to her..."

"Well, before you make any decisions about what we plan to do with her, we have to know for sure."

Carla let out a long, sharp exhale. "What do you propose?"

"We question her. About her activities the past two days. Just like you did with me. See if what she says matches the events we know have taken place. Access her electronic devices—phones, laptops—anything she could be using to contact Coalition members. We need proof."

"She may not come willingly."

Charlotte peered around the area. "There is an alley in the back. Knock her out if you have to and I will help you bring her into the car. If anyone sees us, we can say she passed out and we are taking her to the hospital."

Carla turned towards Charlotte, giving her a small smile. "Not a bad cover story. You're starting to sound like one of us."

Charlotte wasn't sure if she liked that statement or not.

They drove around the rear, parked in an alley spot, and Carla headed inside. Charlotte sat waiting to see if she'd be needed to help. Several minutes later, Carla returned.

Alone.

Once she'd reentered the car, she shook her head. Her face appeared ashen and her hands shook.

"What is it?" Charlotte asked, terrified to know the answer.

"She's dead."

Disbelief froze her for a few moments. "Wait...dead? Jordan?"

"Not only that." Carla turned towards Charlotte, a look of fury in her eyes. "The apartment had been torched." Color returned to her face. "I told her to stay put. This is all my fault...They went after her..."

Before Charlotte could say a word, Carla's phone rang. She removed it from her pocket, her hand squeezing the device as if she would break it.

"Yes," she said after answering. Several moments passed before she spoke again. "I see." More silence. "Of course. I'll be there as soon as I can. It'll be several hours. She'll need to remain safe until then." Carla hung up and turned to Charlotte. "Change of plans."

Without another word, Carla started the car and raced away.

23

October 19th
2:45 p.m.

Sean began to recognize the streets, restaurants, and local haunts of Philly as he entered the city. His destination, Springfield, sat on the west side, so he decided to drive through his hometown. Memories of his youth ignited inside his mind, from baseball games with his parents to visits at the aquarium. He'd spend hours in escape rooms, loving every second of figuring out clues and working with a group of his friends.

Those had been some of his happiest moments. It had been no wonder he'd grown up to be a detective.

As he drove further, other memories surfaced, ones that weren't quite as pleasant. He realized he hadn't been home since his ex-fiancé stood him up at the altar, but the recollection flooded him as he drove past the church they'd been set to marry in.

Yet, that day didn't feel as painful as he thought it would. After everything he'd been through, after all he'd learned about the Triads, about Angellica and Anya's personalities, he realized the two of them really weren't meant to be. And not just because she'd inhabited the body of a killer. They'd tried to rekindle things earlier that year and the whole process made him realize she didn't fit with him.

A different image floated through his mind: one of him and Charlotte in the church instead. The location wasn't right—he mentally moved them to a lakefront or a garden setting—but the notion in and of itself pleased him. It didn't feel forced. It didn't feel rushed. It felt like two halves becoming whole.

Sean shook away the idea. Right now, he'd be happy just to know she was all right.

His phone beeped at him, reminding him of the low battery. In his haste to leave Elaine's after the bombshell of hearing the newest audio clip from Charlotte, he'd forgotten to bring his phone's car charger. The five-hour-and-some-change drive had drained the battery, because he'd constantly played both Mags' message and the audio clip file over and over again. He wasn't sure what he had hoped to accomplish by relistening to them, but just hearing their voices, no matter how grim the subject, gave him comfort.

A longing for time to be turned back six months ached inside him.

Focus, he told himself. *You can't change that. These people need your help in this point in time. And the Triad women need to be stopped, now. All you can do is concentrate on that.*

Passing through the middle of the city, Sean played the Mags message again first. Nothing new on that. Charlotte had been taken or rescued by someone named Carl. Mae would maybe turn traitor against the arson group. He'd asked the precinct for a trace ASAP on the call, but with everyone busy looking for Mags, he didn't know when he'd receive the results.

He switched over to Charlotte's message as his GPS told him he was within two miles of his destination.

I should charge my phone first, he said. He let the audio clip play through anyway while his battery sunk to 5%.

There she was, plain as day, confirming she was in charge of the arson group—the Coalition—and that they were killing Triad members who didn't comply with her rules. No waver in her voice, no stress or strain.

Could Woods and Elaine be right? Could Charlotte just be another one of the "fake personalities" like Mags and Angellica? Had he been fooled once again?

No, he thought. *We all talked about it. It wouldn't make sense for them to claim her as Messiah if she was really a fake person. Although I did always think of her as some kind of Vulcan robot.*

Sean snorted a laugh to himself. Then, he became rock-still as something occurred to him, so much so he almost drove into the car in front of him which had stopped at a light.

"Shit!" he cursed, slamming on his brakes. Luckily, he

stopped short a couple of inches. Readjusting his attention and ignoring the prickle of sweat beneath his arms, Sean pulled over and parked about a block away from his destination at a little café on the corner. Holding his breath, he played the audio clip again.

Nothing happened.

His phone had died.

"Damn!" He exited his vehicle and entered the establishment, noting a couple of electrical outlets near the side wall.

Crossing over, he ordered a coffee to go first, then added a BLT for good measure because he hadn't eaten anything since a drive-thru breakfast sandwich after he'd left Elaine's that morning, then took a seat. A few people sat scattered about the small wooden tables, their conversations low or non-existent as they enjoyed an after-work pit stop. Some sort of soft rock music played through the overhead speakers, mixing with, but not quite covering, the clinks of silverware and whirls of steamers and blenders behind the counter.

Sean plugged his phone into the wall and held it up to his ear, listening to Charlotte's audio clip again as soon as there was enough battery to do so.

"I understand that this path isn't easy for many of you to hear...They are under my rule to dispose of any Triad members who don't follow my orders."

There it was. Plain as day. The reason why something didn't feel right to Sean.

Charlotte was using contractions.

She *never* used contractions.

The only time he'd ever heard her do so he felt like she'd

been lying to him. It had been right after she'd left his place and Violet had been on the loose. He'd asked her if she'd been okay and she'd said, "I'm fine."

That had been right before she'd apparently started helping the Triad women as their Messiah.

So, what did this mean? Was it not really her? Or...an even better possibility was that the speech had been written for her. On purpose? Or coercion?

Sean ended the clip and searched through his contacts to give Woods a call. He wanted another detective's take on this new development.

Before he tapped on his phone to make the call, the door to the café opened. Glancing up at the change in the room, Sean saw a young woman enter. Slim, pretty, with peroxide blonde hair, she stood in the doorway for a few moments, searching the space.

Probably meeting a friend, Sean said. A server appeared and placed his to-go coffee and bagged sandwich in front of him. He was once again about to place his call when someone behind him leaped out of their seat, knocking over their chair, and bolted to the back of the café. The blonde woman standing in the entrance took a step as if to follow, then turned and sprinted back out the front door.

Sean's police senses rose. He grabbed his charger from the wall, stuffed it and his phone into his back pocket, left his food and drink on the table, and took off towards the front entrance after the blonde woman. He got there just in time to see her hair whip around the corner towards the rear of the building.

Sean took off after her, skidding around the edge of the

brick corner. She was fast, already three fourths of the way down the building. He pursued, a little slower than her speed to make sure she didn't realize he was following her and watched as another woman—this one with dark skin and short dark hair—zipped through side exit of the café. The blonde woman pursued, catching her, and pulled her behind the building.

Sean pursued at a full sprint, all guise of caution gone. He gripped the edge of the bricks and swung himself around the final corner to confront the women.

The one being pursued was being pressed against the rear wall of the café. Sean saw a flash of silver metal in the blonde woman's hand.

"Freeze! Police!" Sean ordered, pulling his weapon.

The blonde woman's head whipped around, her eyes wide at the new addition. Sean could see her calculating in those few seconds whether she could kill the woman and still get away, if she should fight against Sean, or if she should just flee.

Sean took a step closer. "Don't," he warned.

The blonde woman's lovely face contorted into a sneer. She retreated away from the victim, her hands held up.

He motioned to her weapon with his own. "Put the knife down."

The sneer turned into a smile.

"Watch—" the woman against the wall cried out.

Too late. A blow struck Sean in the head from behind. The alley danced around him and blurred. He shook his head, stumbling to the side, reaching for a nearby dumpster for support.

"Do it!" he heard someone yell.

"No!" he cried out.

"Help!"

Concentrating with all his willpower, his vision narrowed to a point onto the two women still near the wall. The blonde plunged forward with her knife hand.

Sean lifted his gun and fired.

Two screams, one from the victim, one from behind him.

He swung around, holding out his gun to prevent anyone else from coming at him.

Whoever had hit him currently ran, their body turning the corner of the building and out of sight.

Sean shook his head, once again fighting a brief wave of dizziness. Surer on his feet, he meant to go after the culprit who'd hit him, but a voice called out.

"Please!"

Sean returned his view to the two women. The blonde lay on the ground, sprawled out unceremoniously. A pool of blood glistened around her head. The other one had sunk down into a crouched position, her hand pressed tightly into her stomach.

"Oh God," Sean said, rushing over. Blood seeped from between her fingers. "Keep pressure on it," he told her. She nodded, but then her eyes rolled in their sockets, and she passed out.

"No, no, no!" Sean quickly laid the woman on the ground. With one hand, he pressed against her bleeding abdomen. With the other, he pulled out his phone.

It beeped at him.

Low battery.

Please be enough of a charge left, he internally begged.

Sean dialed 911.

24

October 19th
3:30 p.m.

Charlotte let the steamy water wash over her. She knew they had limited time and she'd promised to keep the shower to around ten minutes, but she allowed herself a count of 120 seconds to just stand there. Her mind a blank slate, she simply breathed, felt the heat of the water, and counted.

They'd driven for about four and a half hours in near silence. Carla had simply told Charlotte they needed to make a stop. Any attempt at conversation had been answered with one syllable words or a comment about having to concentrate on their next move. Not wanting to interrupt the only person who could keep her alive, Charlotte remained quiet.

There had been other food in the backpack Carla brought along and Charlotte didn't hesitate to dig in. Cranberry juice and a couple bottles of water, two egg breakfast sandwiches, two granola bars, a banana, an apple, and some peanut butter crackers. While they drove, Charlotte polished off most of the food, then dozed on and off, wondering about her current predicament.

She couldn't go home.

She couldn't talk to anyone she knew.

She had no idea when she may return to any semblance of a normal life.

This is *normal now,* she currently thought, rubbing the shampoo into her hair. The notion caused a deep longing in her chest. She'd give anything to see a familiar face at this point, chat about a mundane trivial issue like the weather or working late. But a slight sliver of light in her heart burned brightest, indicating her truest desire: to see Sean.

Ideas drifted through her mind, fantasies really, of Carla taking out all the Triad agents they were up against and Charlotte arriving once more to work, then returning to her apartment, and finally diving into Sean's arms. Tears mingled with the shower's water, and she let herself cry for everything she couldn't have anymore.

There was no end in sight. Even if Carla stopped the Coalition and their leader, other Triads knew of her existence and would continue to come after her. More so, they currently believed she'd been responsible for the fires and killings of women all over the world, simply for not agreeing with her "Messiah" vision.

Charlotte let herself wallow for a few more minutes, not caring at the moment about their timetable. She needed to let these thoughts out if there was any chance of her continuing on.

But one thing she knew for sure—she couldn't sit by and do nothing anymore. Her life had been dictated by these women, Carla included, for too long. From this point on, she wanted to be part of the decision-making process. She'd earned that right.

Having even a partial plan gave her a burst of strength. She completed her shower, got dressed—relishing in the clean, new clothes—and exited the showering area. Emerging into the hallway, she found herself in a truck stop, one where Carla had stopped at and dropped her off, telling her she'd return in 20 minutes. She'd given Charlotte some cash, instructed her to take a shower after handing her the backpack full of new clothing, told her to buy food for dinner that night for the two of them, and left without giving Charlotte any other inkling of what Carla meant to do while gone.

No more, Charlotte reinforced within herself. *From now on, I am included.* The whole ordeal had shaken her. She'd never been to a truck stop before. Heck, she hadn't even been on a road trip in ages. It amazed her how content she'd gotten living her day-to-day life, not really seeing the world around her. Even the worldwide journey she'd gone on with Mags a few months ago had felt more like a whirlwind of work more than an excursion.

This is what these women do. They upset people's lives any way they want because they believe their ideas are much more important than everyone else's. Even now, she'd just been left, alone, with only the hope that Carla would return from wherever she'd gone.

Charlotte couldn't do anything about that now. If Carla didn't return, she'd...well, she'd deal with that if that situation occurred. Which was another thing. She didn't like being at the mercy of someone else. Charlotte needed a way to feel secure that plans *did* happen to change, she could make it on her own. After all, she'd been kidnapped while under the watch of Isabella, who was now dead, and Jordan had been found and burned up inside her apartment. Charlotte was quickly losing people who could protect her, so she'd better learn how to protect herself.

Rapidly picking up several items off the truck stop shelves for their dinner later, including two veggie sandwiches, two orange juices, a bag of cheesy popcorn, and a couple of beef jerky sticks, Charlotte then waited just inside the front entrance. It was warmer here in Philadelphia, having traveled southwest, but a strong breeze still kept her hovering indoors.

It took nearly ten more minutes before, Charlotte saw Carla drive up, though she was in a different car, this one a dark green hatchback. Charlotte got in, placing the items in the back seat.

"Something wrong with the last car?" she asked.

"Registered under the same alias as the hotel. Needed to switch it out."

As Carla left the gas station, Charlotte took a deep breath.

"I understand you needed some time to think about our upcoming plans on the drive, but I want to know what is going on. These decisions affect me as well and I have the right to be a part of them."

Carla's gaze flitted towards Charlotte, then onto the road again. "You are absolutely right."

Charlotte, though pleased with the result, felt a little unsure as to why Carla was agreeing. But, she decided not to press her luck.

"So, who called you when we were in Boston, where are we headed, and how long are we planning to stay there?"

Carla pursed her lips for a moment before she answered. "We are heading to Springfield, which is just west of Philadelphia. We have about an hour left of our drive. As for who called me...that is a little more complicated. You need to know other things first. There are certain...details...about myself that I have never revealed to anyone. Not to Isabella or Jordan. Not to anyone else involved in the Triad world."

"And I assume not to me?"

Carla gave a nod, returning to the freeway. "When my Triad betrayed me and murdered my husband, something inside me...broke. I never fully trusted anyone after that point. I created backup procedures and contingencies that no one else knew of. Just in case. Even after joining with Isabella and Jordan, I still couldn't stop initiating these safety-net plans. And now, I'm glad I did, because when you and Isabella were kidnapped, I implemented the first one of these alternate strategies."

"Which was?"

"I found your location using a tracker I'd installed in you shortly after you joined our group."

The words in the sentence had meaning, but Charlotte took several moments to register what she'd actually just heard. "You have a tracker on me?"

"Yes."

A sense of being violated flooded through her. She felt unclean, tainted. "Where?" she demanded.

"Inside your shoulder-blade wound. I inserted it one of the times I cleaned and redressed it for you."

Charlotte reached around her own back as if to claw it out from under her skin. "Get it out. Now!"

"It's already gone. It disintegrates after twenty-four hours of activation."

"That is how you knew where I was for a full day."

Carla nodded.

Anger slithered through her, not only at the invasion of her body, but also remembering what she went through that first day of captivity. "Why did you leave me there for so long?" She held out her hand, exposing her still raw wrist. "They kept me locked up, forced me to read their propaganda, barely fed me, and kept me on the brink of freezing."

"Like I said before, I'm sorry for the delay, but it was necessary."

"Explain to me why." Charlotte could tell Carla was not used to taking orders. She'd never seen the woman so fidgety and reluctant to respond. But she didn't care. Being kept in the dark did not work for her anymore.

"When you didn't show up at the restaurant, I drove around the area, searching for you. You'd gotten rid of your cell phones so I couldn't call. After about half an hour, I knew something had happened. I immediately went home to initiate the tracker. When I arrived, my apartment had been ransacked. I couldn't report the crime, of course, because I didn't want to draw attention to myself. Needless to say, I couldn't stay there anymore.

"Fortunately," she went on, sailing past a speedy little red sports car, "the tracking device wasn't found. I'd hid it and their rummaging hadn't been very thorough. To be honest, it looked more like they'd been waiting a long time and got bored so they rifled through my things."

"You think they were waiting for you to come home?"

Carla nodded and slowed a little when she saw a police car up ahead. "I knew right then that this was a coordinated effort. To have you and Isabella not show up at our meeting point and my apartment invaded at practically the same time...seemed too much of a coincidence."

"You suspected Jordan."

"Not at the time. I contacted her, told her about the situation, and instructed her to stay in her place. I laid low the remainder of the day and that night I tracked you down. I worried they'd find the tracker and set a trap so I didn't want to initiate it too soon. I also figured," she said, clearing her throat, "that if they meant to kill you, you'd already be dead, and a few more hours wouldn't make a difference in finding your body."

Charlotte's anger dribbled away. She had no right to expect Carla to risk her own life to save hers. And yet, these women had brought her into this mess in the first place. She just assumed they would keep her safe.

Except Isabella told her they could only do their best. They were only three women, after all, against a multitude of possible Triad members. She'd even told Charlotte there were three attempts to either take her or kill her before Isabella and the two others even revealed themselves.

It was not their fault, Charlotte reminded herself. *Truth started this months ago when she alerted the Triads that I am the Messiah.* From that moment forward, she'd had a target on her. Carla and the others were simply doing damage control.

"What happened when you turned the tracker on?" Charlotte asked, returning to the conversation at hand.

"I located you at the warehouse. That night, I surveilled the area. They had tight security. I knew a frontal approach wouldn't work. And besides," she said, pausing for a moment. "I wanted to make sure that if Isabella was alive, I could save her, too."

Charlotte's gut tightened. Maybe she'd been wrong about what she'd heard... "And?"

"I couldn't find her. There were no other areas where anyone was being held. Your tracking device came through loud and clear, so they weren't jamming any signals."

"Do you think they took her someplace else?"

Carla shrugged. "I don't see the point. There would be no reason to keep her. In their eyes, she's just someone in their way while getting to you."

Charlotte's eyes stung with tears. "I had hoped... perhaps..." She let out a sigh. "I heard one of my kidnappers in the van say to remove the 'other' one and burn the body once they had me. I suppose I still thought maybe she had made it out somehow, but if you could not find her and she has not contacted you..." The full weight of the idea of Isabella being dead, especially with Jordan gone, hit Charlotte harder than she expected. There really wasn't anyone left except Carla. How could this one woman keep her safe?

"We cannot do this alone," Charlotte said.

"Agreed."

Surprise hit her. "Really?"

"I may have not ever fully trusted anyone, but I'm not an *idiota*. From the first time Isabella approached me, I knew we were working on borrowed time. The Triads were too much for just the two of us. Even adding Jordan to our group, we had such a slim chance of making a real difference. But I was full of anger at the time and believed that any chance at stopping *any* of those murderers was worth a shorter life span." She went silent for a moment. "Then we heard about you."

"And you decided to use me to help stop the Triads," Charlotte said, filling in the rest.

"Not at first."

Several moments passed. "Meaning?" Charlotte asked. Her hair had almost fully dried since her shower, and she began to braid it over one shoulder.

"Isabella pitched you as leverage—a way to force the Triads into following our plan by using you as a hostage. She didn't believe in you, not right away. None of us did. It had been so long since we'd heard of a Messiah claim...it really was too incredible to imagine. So instead, we came up with a strategy to take you and use your image for our own purposes."

"Seems as though you were not the only ones with that

plan..."

"Exactly. The Coalition has done just that."

"What changed your minds about me?"

Carla's caramel-toned cheeks flushed. "I did. I reexamined your background, reinvestigated you. I did it to find a weakness to exploit, in case our plan wouldn't work, but I found nothing. You fit all the criteria as if the Book had written it specifically for you. I'm not usually one for sentimental things, but I began to believe. In you."

Charlotte wasn't sure what to say. She'd known Carla considered her the Messiah, but she didn't realize she'd convinced Isabella and Jordan of that fact as well. Somehow, she felt a touch uncomfortable with the level of certainty coming from Carla.

Charlotte didn't think of herself as anything special, not for these women. The requirements given in the Book meant nothing to her. A little eerie, perhaps, but she didn't believe in destiny that way. And yet she knew how powerful faith could be. That's why she chose to claim herself as Messiah in the first place—to get these women to stop because they *would* follow her based on their devotion.

"So, we changed our plan," Carla went on. "And during that time, I began to search for other Triad women who might join our cause. Isabella and Jordan didn't know. They only wanted to stop the Triad women. But I wondered, if other rogue agents knew we were working with you, maybe they would be more...how do you say the word...pliable to our way of thinking."

"Did you discover anyone?" Charlotte tucked the braid

behind her, adjusting her head against the headrest.

"I only started this a couple weeks ago, so no, I haven't. But I knew a woman from before I joined with Isabella and Jordan. I met her shortly after I worked with my Triad group down in Brazil."

"How did you find her?"

"She found me. She'd found out about the order to kill my husband. Apparently, she still tracked the progress of her old Triad, which became my *new* Triad." Carla glanced over and saw the look of confusion on Charlotte's face. "She, Olivia, was a third before I was. She's about fifty-five years old now. She quit her Triad thirty-five years ago."

Carla's tone quieted. "She thought she could warn me, to protect my husband."

Charlotte recalled how Carla had lost her husband, which was the reason she'd left her Triad, since they were the ones who decided to murder him. "But it was too late?"

"Yes and no. Olivia got to me before my husband's death." Carla cleared her throat. "But I was in my alternate persona, who had no idea what this woman spoke of. Olivia tried to protect my husband but failed. So, she waited until she knew I was my true self and approached me. By then the damage had been done. I'd had my suspicions about my Triad's involvement in his death and she confirmed them."

Charlotte wondered about the story. "If you, as thirds, always follow orders, why did Olivia resist and leave her own Triad?"

"She got pregnant."

Charlotte's eyes widened. "Is pregnancy a reason to quit?"

"Not in the eyes of a Triad. Your alternate self would raise any children, if you didn't choose to terminate the pregnancy. You see, she wanted to remain pregnant, as herself. Triads don't let thirds stay in their true form. So, the only way for her to raise any children herself was to leave the Triad. The only way to do *that* was to not let them know about the pregnancy and escape. She faked her own death."

Charlotte shook her head. "Everything I have learned so far leads me to believe you have all been willing participants. Why fight about leaving her in her true persona?"

"The Book doesn't allow it. And the alternative is death. Once you join the group, you don't leave. Ever. Unless you're retired. Some Triads don't like killing their thirds if they don't have to. They employ...other methods to keep them. Don't forget, killing always leaves a trail. If too many deaths occur, it could expose the Triads. That was one thing they couldn't let occur."

"So, this woman, Olivia, the two of you kept in touch?"

"Yes."

Charlotte was starting to fill in the pieces. "And that is who we are going to meet?"

"No." Carla glanced over at Charlotte. "We are going to see her daughter. She's being targeted by the Triads."

Charlotte stammered, "You are taking us *to* Triad members?"

"We have no choice. We need help. Olivia is well connected. She will have supplies, safe houses, new IDs, all of it. But she needs to make sure her daughter is safe first. Then, she'll help us."

Suddenly the car felt very small. Charlotte's chest tightened.

"I knew if I told you," Carla said, "you'd resist."

"You are *completely* accurate on that statement!"

Carla banged her hand against the steering wheel, startling Charlotte. "Charlotte, I don't know what else to do to protect you. Everyone is gone. Jordan, Isabella…We have no one else we can turn to. Olivia risked her own life to try to protect my husband. She has been there for me for a long time. I have to help her daughter."

"What about me? I cannot exactly help in a 'rescue' attempt."

"I plan to drop you at a safe location provided by Olivia. Once I get her daughter, we'll return for you."

"Then what?"

Carla gave her a meaningful look. "You said you wanted to be a part of the planning process? Well, I hope you can come up with a good plan."

Instant regret at her own words filled her. And yet, they needed a strategy. Carla was flying by the seat of her pants and had no clue what to do next, except hide.

But how long could they do that? Even worse, the Coalition intended to move forward with whatever their scheme was in using Charlotte's fake speech. She and Carla needed to find out about that plan and the only way to do that was to be in Boston, where the Coalition congregated.

Charlotte spoke. "After we pick up the daughter and make sure she is safe, we are going to return to Boston."

Carla furrowed her forehead, crossing lanes to make sure

she took the exit ramp towards Philadelphia. "That is the last place we should go. There are too many agents working there, and all looking for you, I'm sure. I can't hide you safely for very long."

A strategy began to form inside Charlotte's mind. "Maybe hiding is not what we need to do…"

25

October 19th

4:00 p.m.

Sean yawned and peered down into his empty coffee cup. The hospital, like most hospitals he'd been to, had watery coffee that seemed to perk him up for about ten minutes at a time. Another pang of longing for Mags' coffee filtered through him. She'd sounded so scared in that message on his phone. He really wondered if she may not return at all.

Not that he understood the intricacies of what the Triads did to create these fake personas, but it sounded pretty complicated. And something that had to be maintained. Without help, Mags would eventually disappear.

A sense of pride swelled inside him and smiled. *Only Mags*

would use the last remaining moments of her time on this planet to try and help take these Triad members down.

Sean only hoped that the tidbits she'd given him could be put to good enough use to do just that.

The woman in the hospital bed in front of him moaned.

Sean stood up from the chair and took a step forward but didn't want to crowd her. Eventually her eyelids fluttered, and she opened her eyes. The look of fear and confusion on her face was unmistakable.

"It's okay, miss," he said, holding a hand up to show he meant no harm.

"I'm..." she said, her voice groggy. "I'm in the hospital?"

"Yes. You were...attacked behind the café. I called 911 and an ambulance picked you up."

She blinked several times, as if putting the pieces together. Her eyesight roamed the room, taking in the heart rate monitor, the sterile environment. Slowly, she slid her hands down to her side. "I was stabbed." The words came as a statement instead of a question.

"Yeah."

With slow movements, she gingerly pressed down on her abdomen. "I don't feel stabbed."

"Probably the painkillers."

"And you," she said, turning her head towards him. "You were there. Police, right?"

Sean nodded and moved closer. "My name is Sean Trann. I'm a detective from Boston."

A wrinkled brow. "Boston?"

"I'm in town on...business. I saw you get chased from the

café and followed you."

Soft beeps from the nearby machine and a gentle hiss from the air vents filled the space for a few moments.

"That woman…" Suddenly her eyes opened wide, and she frantically peered around the room. "What happened to her?"

Sean internally cringed. "She wouldn't stop, so I shot her. She was pronounced dead by the paramedics." He hadn't shot his gun in the line of duty very many times, but in the past six months, the number had increased dramatically. Still, this woman only put him at three who'd been fatally injured from his own weapon. It wasn't something he took lightly, but the grogginess from being hit over the head and the worry over the stabbed victim had blocked any ability to concentrate on the blonde woman's death.

"And the other one?"

Sean rubbed the back of his head. He'd gotten a small lump, but the EMT's had checked him out and said he seemed fine, not concussed or anything permanent. "She got away. But I gave the local police a description. They'll want to get a statement from you. I told them I'd call when you woke up."

The woman struggled to sit up. "That's nice of you to have stayed with me."

Sean cleared his throat. "Well, when the hospital contacted your insurance company, there wasn't any emergency contact listed."

"My parents live out of state, and I just took my girlfriend's name, well, 'ex' girlfriend's name off the list. Guess I forgot to update it."

"I wanted to make sure you were all right and to help the

police catch the other woman who did this. I'll give them a call now."

The woman shook her head. "They won't catch her," she mumbled.

Sean narrowed his eyes. "Why not? Do you know who she is?"

With a snort she said, "You wouldn't believe me if I told you." She let out a sigh. "Thanks for staying, really, but I'll be all right. I just want to talk to the doctor."

"I understand. I'm...I'm sorry I couldn't stop her before she hurt you."

The woman waved him away. "You saved my life by stopping her at all. I'm sure she would have left me for dead."

"If you're in any kind of trouble, you really should tell the police when they get here, Miss..."

"Oni," she said. "You can call me Oni. And yeah, I'll keep that in mind."

Sean didn't quite believe her, but he couldn't press the subject. Who knew why she wanted to protect the women who came after her? Maybe they were family or previous friends or something. Maybe they were involved in something illegal.

"Well, Oni, I'm just glad I was there. Take care of yourself, will you?"

She nodded and gave a sad smile.

Sean felt for her as he walked out of the room. As a cop, he understood the ins and outs of the corrupt and criminal. But sometimes, they were just good people who got in over their heads and couldn't see a way out. Not that it excused their choices, but the world could be a very desperate place sometimes, and desperation could cause people to panic into making poor decisions.

Shaking those thoughts away, he concentrated instead on the tasks at hand. He would notify the local police that Oni had woken up—not that she really wanted to report anything to them, but Sean had told the authorities he'd let them know. Then, he wanted to check in with Elaine and Woods. Elaine would probably have already spoken with some of the bunker women, and he felt curious about any information they might have given her. Woods, like himself, had probably only gotten to Rochester about an hour ago and he wondered if he'd met up with "Zack Attack" yet. The knowledge about where the audio clips came from could be extremely useful in tracking down whoever might have an idea about both Charlotte's whereabouts and her involvement with the Triads.

After that, he'd return to the street with the café where he'd initially been going—following up on the Roswall Corporation listed on that block. He realized, a little too late, that it was the weekend, and the company may not be open until Monday. But he hoped if that were the case, he could find out who ran the place and track down their home address and talk to them personally tomorrow. He'd already decided that with the long drive and after getting hit on the head, he wouldn't mind staying overnight. A hotel room with crappy cable movies, an order of Chinese food, and a break from the craziness that was his life sounded perfect right now.

Reaching into his back pocket to place the first call, Sean internally cursed when his hand came out empty.

My phone must have slipped out of my pocket in Oni's

room, he thought. Turning on his heel, Sean strode down the corridor and stuck his head into the open doorway, knocking lightly to announce his presence.

A woman, wearing a white lab coat, stood next to Oni's bed.

Probably her doctor, Sean said. He waved and Oni smiled. "Don't mean to interrupt," he said, pointing to the chair across the room. He could see his phone lying on the floor next to it. "I just dropped my..." He trailed off as the doctor turned towards him.

It was the woman who'd bashed him over the head and fled the alleyway behind the café.

The whole room seemed to freeze for a moment.

"Detective?" Oni said, breaking the silence.

Sean reached for his weapon, but then realized he'd left it in the car in the lockbox as this hospital did not permit firearms. Since he was out of his jurisdiction, he didn't want to push the statute, but at this moment, he wished he had.

"Step away from her," he told the woman in the lab coat.

She simply stood there, as if assessing the situation.

Oni struggled again to sit up further, her eyes wide with alarm. "Is she from the alleyway?" she asked, her voice tight.

Sean nodded.

"You're a detective," the fake doctor said.

"I said step away," Sean repeated. He moved towards her but stopped when he saw a syringe in her hand.

"Who's faster?" the fake doctor asked. An eeriness crept over him at the calmness in her voice.

She's a professional, Sean thought. *Same kind of look as the blonde woman in the alley. I have to give her a way out, otherwise she'll just continue and take her chances.*

"You're right," he said, remembering his negotiating tactics 101—never say "no" and make them think they have the power. "But you'll have an issue with getting away."

"True." Still so calm, still so smooth.

"So, what do we do here?"

The fake doctor stood for several more seconds. "I leave."

Sean's jaw tightened. "You assaulted me in that alleyway."

"If you were going to arrest me, you would have done so already. Which tells me..." she looked him up and down. "You don't belong here." She said the words in a sort of sing-song fashion which made his skin crawl.

Sean saw Oni's eyes widen as well, but then they narrowed. "Screw you!" she screamed.

The fake doctor, completely caught off guard, whipped her head towards Oni.

Oni grabbed the syringe and shoved it at the woman.

Sean ran forward, clearing the space in mere moments, and tackled the fake doctor.

The syringe flew through the air. It landed on the windowsill. The woman underneath Sean squirmed and twisted. He was having a hard time holding her still.

"Someone help us!" Oni shouted.

Within moments, a nurse entered, gave a little shriek, and left.

The fake doctor got a hand free and smashed her fist into Sean's throat. Pain lanced through his vocal cords, and he couldn't catch his breath.

While gagging, he reached over next to him, feeling the edges of the IV stand. He grabbed it, lifted it up, and smashed the metal onto the fake doctor's face.

Dazed, she dropped her guard. Sean flipped her over and held her hands behind her. He yanked down the cord from the curtains. Tying her hands together, he turned her onto her back. Her eyes had cleared from the glancing blow and the coldness in them made the hair on his neck stand up.

"You've no idea who you're messing with," she hissed.

At that moment a few hospital staff and two security guards entered.

Sean stood, holding his hands up, and ID'ing himself, coughing a little on the words, his throat still sore.

After a few moments, the guards escorted the fake doctor from the room and one of the real doctors checked out Sean's throat, saying there'd been no permanent damage, then spoke with Oni. She told them the fake doctor hadn't done anything to her, but then nodded in the direction of the syringe on the windowsill.

"She said she was giving me something to stave off any infections," she said. "I had no idea she wasn't my doctor."

"Well, I really *am* your doctor and I'm giving you a sedative. Don't worry, it's mild. I just think it would be good if you got some rest after all this."

One of the guards returned. "The police will be here soon."

"Can I make a phone call first?" Oni asked. "I want to let my mom know I'm okay."

"Yeah, sure, that's fine." He glanced at Sean. "You okay to stay with her until the police come?"

"Not a problem." Sean didn't want to leave that room until he knew Oni would be safe.

One of the doctors gave Oni her personal effects. "Keep the call brief, okay? You just came out of surgery for that knife wound. You need sleep."

Oni nodded, pulling her phone from her purse.

The doctor left, speaking with the guard about how the police could come tomorrow, that this woman needed to rest, while closing the door behind them.

"Holy shit," Oni said, once it was just the two of them. "That's twice you saved my life."

"Most people don't need saving even once," Sean retorted. "You want to tell me what's going on?"

"Uh, no. No thanks, I mean. I just...I don't want to get anyone involved."

"The police are going to come and question you. Two attempts on your life in one day is going to bring up a lot of questions."

Sean could see the nervousness plastered across her face. "Yeah...yeah I suppose it will. I don't really have any answers for them."

"At least," Sean said slowly, "none you want to give."

"What I really want to do is call my mom and then close my eyes. I've had a long day." She gave a weak smile.

Sean hesitated. He knew he had things to do, people to call, a place to visit, but he really found it difficult to leave her alone right now. "I'll step outside, but I'm not going anywhere until the police arrive." He held up his hand in defense. "I don't know what the problem is, but they are just going to want to help."

"They can't." All the air seemed to rush out of her, and her eyes turned a touch glassy. "I was stupid. My mom was right. I thought...I thought I could cover everything up. Thought they wouldn't find me."

"*Who* wouldn't find you?"

Oni shook her head. A strange half smirk formed on her face. Her words came out a little slurred. "It doesn't matter. My mom said someone was going to come and help me, but it's too late. I'm already on their radar. I won't get away."

Sean wondered what was wrong with her, why she was suddenly babbling, but then he saw the IV. *The sedative,* he thought.

She held up her phone. "Can you call my mom? I don't remember how this thing is with all the buttons and tapping it's like a weird game where I can't make any sense of it." The words poured from her mouth like racing droplets over a waterfall.

Sean stepped forward quickly and caught the phone as it tipped from her hand.

Oni's eyes cleared a little, but the same weird grin remained plastered on her face. "Can you just tell her where I am? Her friendCarlaissupposed to find me but she can't cuzI'mhere. My mom is under 'O' in the contacts with the names of the peoplethatIcall. You know. The people."

"I understand," Sean said gently.

Oni smiled wider and then her eyelids fluttered closed.

Sean exited the room and saw one of the guards coming towards him.

"Hey!" the guard called. He'd been one of the individuals who'd helped take care of the false doctor. He looked like he was fresh out of high school. "I guess the doc spoke to the cops and told them not to come until tomorrow. But you can go if you want. I'll hang out here until my shift ends. Don't worry, I'll check ID's before anyone goes into the room, but they arrested the lady who went after her, so I'm sure the patient will be all right."

Sean hesitated a moment, wishing he could do more, but the situation seemed under control. All he really wanted was to plop his head down on a pillow and sleep for ten hours. Instead, he held up Oni's phone. "She asked me to call her mother and let her know where she is," Sean answered. "I'll step outside. When I'm done, I'll leave the phone at the nurses' station, in case she wakes up and asks where it is."

"I'm on it," the guard said. He stood next to the door with his arms crossed.

"And one more thing," Sean said.

"Yeah?"

"Thanks for helping me out in there. You did a good job."

The young guard beamed. "Thank you, sir."

Sean slapped him on the shoulder and walked away. Once outside, he powered up Oni's phone, found the contact marked "O," and called the number.

"Please tell me she's there," the woman named "O" said when she answered after the first ring.

"Hello, ma'am," Sean said, using his most professional tone. "My name is Detective Sean Trann. Your daughter is all right, but she was taken to the hospital today after being attacked. She asked me to call you and let you know. She's at Springfield Hospital."

Silence.

"Ma'am? Are you there?"

Click. Dial tone.

<h1 style="text-align:center">26</h1>

October 19th
4:15 p.m.

Crossing the Delaware River, Charlotte took in the sight of the Philadelphia skyline. The sun hung low in the sky, about an hour from sunset, and a band of reddish-orange clung to the horizon like a scattered pile of fallen autumn leaves. She'd never been to this city, since most of her life consisted of living on the West Coast, but the sight reminded her of growing up in Portland, Oregon after they moved there when she'd turned ten.

This is where Sean grew up, she thought. The similarity between both cities constructed along a river made her feel connected to him. She wondered how he was, if he'd become worried about her yet after her voicemail. What she'd told him concerned her. Had she revealed too much? At the time, she'd simply needed to confide in someone; even though she hadn't specifically said she'd be helping the Triads, she did feel the need to let him know she wouldn't be around for a while.

We could have been spending the weekend together. Instead, she'd claimed herself the Messiah of the Triads, gotten kidnapped by a bunch of arsonists, made to give a fake speech incriminating herself, left without much food or heat for two days, then dramatically rescued by Carla only to be hunted down at the hotel and forced once again to go on the run.

She wondered if she should chance calling him, to tell him she still couldn't meet up. At some point, he'd not only worry, he'd try to find her and instead discover her missing. But truthfully, she knew the desire to place a call revolved around her wanting to hear his voice. He would wait. She'd requested time, and he would respect that. Especially for a case.

Besides, she needed to focus on her and Carla's two-part plan.

Well, mostly *her* plan. Carla hadn't seemed too keen on the idea.

"You want to what?" Carla had asked her half an hour earlier in the car.

"I want to make another video. Send it to the rest of the Triad members. You can do that, correct?"

"Well, yes, but...*ay Dios mio* WHY?"

Charlotte pulled one of the beef jerky sticks from the truck stop bag. "I have been thinking about the conversation I had with Mae. That speech they had me record. The fact that there were inconsistencies in my speech pattern *and* the fact that whoever is in charge of the Coalition is setting them up makes me think there is something more to this."

Carla had clucked her tongue against the roof of her mouth. "Just because the speech said you were in charge of the Coalition doesn't mean someone is setting them up. And it doesn't mean you have to expose yourself by creating a new video."

"I believe it does." Charlotte snapped off a bite of beef jerky. Excitement came through her tone. "Imagine this from the point of view of an average Triad member. First, six months ago, Truth announces I am the Messiah. That claim has not transpired for seventy-five years. It would create doubt in most of these women, and rightfully so.

"As time passed," Charlotte had continued, "the Triad members would have split into believers, non-believers, and those who simply wanted to continue doing what they were doing, without any outside influence."

"I can understand that."

"Next, the first video filmed with Isabella. I put myself out there, asserting my position as Messiah. They have now seen me. They have heard I fit the 'Messiah' criteria. The believers are now set, the non-believers are now resistant, and the ones who did not care are starting to listen, because what I say will affect them."

"That is what we wanted," Carla said. "Our original plan. To get them accustomed to you and turn as many as we could towards non-violence."

"Exactly. Except the next speech they heard was of me

claiming violence toward any resistance by publicly exposing them through the pursuit of the Coalition. *Opposite* of the whole secrecy of the Triads. And attacking our own? The Messiah is supposed to guide, not dominate."

Carla had nodded, knowingly. "They set you up to be a tyrant."

"Precisely. With the Coalition as my weapon of choice."

"And if the Coalition is attached to you..."

"...when I 'fall,' they would fall with me."

"Which means the members of the Coalition will no longer be needed." Carla shook her head in disbelief. "So, someone *is* setting up the Coalition."

"And I do not think the Coalition followers know."

Carla let out a sharp breath. "Which brings us to the second part of your *loca* plan. You want to contact Mae."

Charlotte finished chewing the last bite of jerky and tucked the wrapper back into the bag. "Based on the doubts I told her, I truly believe Mae will see the plan to eliminate her and the others in her group, if she has not already. Remember, even though she is not Mags, she still has Mags' intelligence. Because of this, she will be forced to choose a side. I believe, logically, she will have to see that she cannot fight against me when her leader is setting her up."

Over the following thirty minutes they discussed what Charlotte might say in her next video, throwing out idea after idea, fine-tuning everything with precise words and inflections.

Once they felt satisfied, Carla finished with, "I still think you're crazy."

Maybe, Charlotte currently thought as their car finished

crossing the river and drove through the eastern part of the city. But maybe "crazy" was exactly what they needed. Up until this point they'd done everything to stay out of the spotlight, as expected. *So let us do the unexpected.*

They pulled up to their hotel, checked in, and spoke briefly in the lobby.

"Remember," Carla told her, "don't answer the phone, the door, nothing. If you think you may have been compromised, here." She handed Charlotte a burner phone. "I picked this up when you were showering at the truck stop. My number is the only one programmed into it."

"Got it."

Carla turned to leave when her other phone rang. She twisted around and motioned for Charlotte to join her down the hall a bit, away from the elevators and any other patrons.

"I just arrived," Carla said into the phone. Her eyes widened. "I understand...which hospital?...all right....yes...the police..." Carla's face tightened. "I will deal with it...yes, him too...I swear. I'll be there within the next half hour. I'll call you when I have her."

Carla hung up.

"Hospital?" Charlotte asked, her mouth dry.

Carla didn't speak for a few moments, as if trying to decide what to say. "*Ay, si,* yes, um that was Olivia. She just got a call informing her that her daughter was admitted to Springfield Hospital. She'd been stabbed. A det—officer saved her life."

"Oh my...her mother was right? Triads?"

Carla grimaced. "Olivia wasn't sure. But...the police are involved. That can't happen." Carla gripped Charlotte's arm.

"If Oni talks…"

Charlotte understood. No exposure. "If the Triads are already after her, will they send someone else?"

"Because they are collaborating, I believe so, yes. And as soon as possible. Even within the hospital itself, if necessary."

"Go," Charlotte urged her. "Go get her and bring her back here."

Carla rubbed her forehead. "I don't know if that will be possible. A stab wound…she will need rest and treatment. Changing of her bandages, checking on her stiches, painkillers, making sure there aren't any infections." Carla had begun to pace.

A lump formed inside Charlotte's throat, but she forced herself to speak. "Let me get those things."

Carla stopped mid-stride. "What?"

"I am positive there is a place around here that will have what we need—a pharmacy of some type. I will ask at the front desk. I simply need some money. I will then meet you here after."

"Charlotte, you are still being hunted."

"The likelihood anyone will be looking for me is slim." She forced a smile even though her gut tumbled like an offset dryer. "I will be quick, but this young woman, she needs help." Charlotte straightened. "Let me do something to assist."

Carla waited a beat, then nodded, placing a few twenties in Charlotte's hand and the second room key. "Remember, call if *anything* seems out of place."

"I will. I promise."

Carla squeezed Charlotte's hand, then took off briskly

towards the lobby entrance.

Charlotte took in a deep breath and headed for the front desk to ask for directions to the nearest pharmacy.

27

October 19th
5:00 p.m.

After returning the phone to the nurses' station, Sean found a decent-looking hotel and checked in for the night. He'd debated whether he wanted to go to the address of the website company, but after getting whacked in the back of the head, punched in the throat, and saving someone's life not once, but twice today, he had no energy left for anything else. He hadn't even called in to check on Woods and Elaine. The will to do so just couldn't be found.

Instead, he ordered Chinese food, found a good action film on cable, and fell onto the king-sized bed. His thoughts drifted as he lay there, dozing in and out of sleep. A beeping woke him.

"Oh yeah," he muttered. "My phone." He'd charged it somewhat in the hospital lobby as he'd waited for the results of Oni's surgery, but once he'd gone to her room, he'd forgotten to plug it in again. Being an older model, his battery didn't hold a charge like it used to.

"Should probably get a new phone when I get home," he muttered.

The simplicity of that sentence lodged in his brain like a splinter. That should not be an important grouping of words. Not a big deal. A task you'd do every so often. Get a new phone. But the idea of returning to Boston to do something so ordinary struck him. He didn't have a simple life anymore. He wondered if he ever could again.

What is the point of this? he asked himself. *What the hell do I think I can accomplish?* The Triads were many, spread across the world, and he was part of a tiny group. Even Woods, who'd been working on this for several years, with multiple others helping him, had gotten betrayed and his people wiped out. And Elaine—did she plan to write a story exposing the Triads? Did she think they wouldn't come after her if they got a whiff of her intent?

To what end? Even if a story *did* occur, it would be the aftermath of what happened six months ago. Phone calls about suspicious activity, citizens who thought they might be sleeper agents, false claims from fake Triad people who just wanted attention...

Meanwhile the real Triad agents would quietly close shop again for a while, disappearing without any problem doing so.

The capability of these women to survive could be seen in their elaborate bunker six months ago. Where all this had started. Where he'd almost lost Charlotte the first time.

Sean's thoughts lingered on her. She'd been named their Messiah in that bunker. He couldn't imagine someone telling him that basically their whole religious group believed he was some mythical savior to their people. And yet she had to deal with that. Their entire institution believed in her...

...or didn't. Doubters could be expected.

But maybe that was why...

Sean sat up and replayed the message she'd left him three nights ago, focusing on some key things she'd said.

"*I am involved in something...confidential.*"

"*I do believe, though, that I am doing the right thing.*"

"*I believe I will contribute to make the world a better place.*"

Sean thought about her words. Though he'd known Charlotte a little over a year, and he'd only truly gotten to know her well these past few months, he felt like her understood her. Though not impulsive and mostly logical, she would still try something new if she believed it would help the situation.

Like venting to me over a few beers, he thought with a smile.

Independent and a force to be reckoned with, sure, but also willing to put in the work. Even if it was hard or scary.

Sean tapped his fingers together across his chest and stared up at the hotel ceiling. *Hard or scary. Like claim herself as Messiah to get them to stop killing?*

The notion sunk into his mind like a weight into wax.

"That makes sense," he said out loud.

He then listened to the two audio clips from the website, the shorter one first.

"...confirm her claim. I am the Triad Messiah."

"Her" must have been Truth, the woman who led Sean to Charlotte's whereabouts to save her. Truth had believed in Charlotte so much, she must have announced it to the other members. And now Charlotte was accepting this claim for them all.

He played the newest clip next.

"I understand that this path isn't easy for many of you to hear. Those who resist will meet with the same fate as any who disobey my orders. You have heard of the fires. You have heard of the Coalition. They are under my rule to dispose of any Triad members who don't follow my orders."

These words were the clear-cut ideals of a ruthless dictator. They didn't lend any credibility to her previous voicemail, which said she wanted to contribute to make the world a better place.

And the contractions. Definitely not like Charlotte.

The only likely conclusion? Someone wrote that speech for her.

And who had last been with Charlotte?

Mae.

It all came down to her. Sean could spend all his time tracking this website person or getting more evidence about Triad movement from Elaine, but the truth was, he knew who he had to find.

Mae.

And he had a phone number to do just that.

Waiting wasn't the easiest thing in the world, but he'd check in the morning and push a little more for getting a trace on Mae's number. However, even with a push, the tracers said they probably couldn't get to his request until Monday. Two days felt like a lifetime.

In the meantime, he'd get some sleep, call Woods and Elaine in the morning for updates, and then pursue the Roswall Corporation.

With slumber beckoning, Sean laid back down and tapped on his phone to close out his messages, but instead accidentally played the message from Mags again. Afraid of inadvertently deleting it—he could never remember if he needed to press seven or nine to erase or save it—he let it play through.

"...That's all I can give you. I hope it's enough....Oh yeah! The kidnapper or rescuer or whoever who took C is named Carl—OW!"

The message ended just as abruptly as before.

Sean hoped Mags was okay. He knew she'd suffered from migraines and from the sounds of the message, it sounded like one had already been building for a while.

Suddenly, Sean bolted into a sitting position as if stuck in the spine with a porcupine quill.

"Whoever took Charlotte is named Carl...ow."

Breath racing in and out, Sean said the words out loud again.

"Whoever took Charlotte is named Carl...!"

What if it isn't Carl? These Triad members are almost exclusively women. What if it's Car-la and the "a" got cut off from the exclamation of pain?

Normally, that wouldn't have been such an exciting revelation, but Oni, in the hospital, had mentioned her mother was sending a friend...CARLA...to come get her.

Puzzle pieces began to click into place in his brain.

Oni had been attacked by two random women, one who even pretended to be a doctor to make sure she got her kill. She said she couldn't talk about it, that Sean wouldn't believe her, that the police couldn't help, and that she'd messed up covering her tracks.

"Oh my God," he said, adrenaline spiking inside him. "Oni was attacked by Triad agents. I gotta help her."

Leaping from the bed, Sean shoved his shoes onto his feet and grabbed the jacket from the side table. With a quick turn, he unplugged and grabbed his phone, then opened the door.

"Shit!" the person on the other side of it yelped.

"Oh, sorry!" Sean exclaimed.

The delivery person blew her bangs off her forehead. "You scared the *crap* out of me."

"Sorry, sorry." Scents of spiced chow mein noodles and chicken fried rice hit him, and his stomach growled. "I'm just leaving," he said, his belly gurgling in protest.

"But..." the young woman said, holding up a plastic bag with his food order.

"Oh, yeah, of course." Sean dug out his wallet from his pocket, pulled out two twenties for the twenty-two-dollar meal, and handed them over. "Keep the change."

Her eyes lit up. "Oh, wow, thanks!" She handed over the food and moved down the hallway, as if worried Sean might realize his high tip mistake and take it back.

Dropping the food just inside the hotel room, Sean followed, closing the door behind him. After a short ride down the three flights in the elevator, Sean bolted to his car and drove once again to the hospital.

28

October 19th

5:15 p.m.

Oni heard a voice through her sedated sleep.

"I want to see my sister," the voice demanded. It sounded feminine, with some sort of accent. Spanish maybe?

A man responded. "Ma'am, you need ID that shows you are related. You don't even have the same last name." Oni heard him snort. "And, no offense, but you don't exactly *look* like sisters, and I'm not supposed to let anyone in except the doctors."

Oni's eyelids fluttered open.

"Of course we don't look alike or have the same last name, you *idiota,*" the woman's voice continued. "She's mixed. We have different dads. She's my *half*-sister."

Oni became fully alert. She didn't *have* any siblings. Was this another Triad woman trying to get in to kill her? But why make such a public fuss?

"Look, I'm sorry..."

"Carla," the woman said loudly. "My name is Car-la. And I have a *right* to see my sister who has just been *stabbed*!"

The name registered in Oni's mind.

Carla.

The guard, sounding panicky said, "Well, she's sleeping right now anyway and visiting hours are almost over so I'll find you the doctor and he can chat with you about your...your sister."

Oni cried out, "Is that Carla? Let her in!"

"I *told* you," Carla said. "Now get out of my way, *cabrón!*" A lovely Latina woman pushed her way into the room and rushed over to Oni's side. "Oh, *hermana*, mom told me about what you went through. Are you all right?"

Even though she didn't understand the Spanish words, relief flooded through Oni more powerful than any painkiller. "Yeah," she said, her eyes filling with tears, "I'm okay. Considering."

Carla whipped her head around to the guard. "Do you *mind*?" she snapped at him.

The young man cowered and left the room, closing the door gently behind him.

Carla straightened up, her entire demeanor changing in an instant. Instead of a loud, scared visitor she appeared exactly as her mom had described—coolheaded, yet someone not to be trifled with.

"Are you really all right?" Carla asked, her tone even.

Oni nodded. "A bit sleepy. They gave me a sedative after a Triad agent, posing as a doctor, came after me."

Carla folded her hands in front of her. "Whatever you've done to upset them, it appears to be important enough to send two agents after you. And to do so in such a quick manner, in public, without a real plan of escape? Someone is desperate to remove your presence from this world."

Fear encroached on Oni's mind. "She got arrested. The woman who came after me here. And the first one, a detective shot and killed her. He saved my life. He called for an ambulance. So, I'm okay now, right?" Oni was ranting, but she couldn't help it. It felt so good to talk to someone who knew about all this Triad stuff. She hadn't realized how lonely and isolated she'd really become during the past few years. She'd held onto the secret of the Triads, keeping it quiet from her friends, girlfriends, even her adoptive parents.

Carla placed a hand gently on Oni's and the tears came. She sobbed for a few minutes, just letting the last few years slide out of her like ink from a broken pen.

"They know you are here," Carla continued, as if Oni hadn't just broken down in front of her. "You can't stay."

Oni let out a sound like a cross between a scoff and a laugh. "Oh yeah, sure, I'll just get up and go. You know I just got stabbed, right?"

Carla's face hardened and Oni shut her mouth. She had a bad habit of snapping at people when scared or defensive.

"I don't know what your mother has told you. I don't

know what you did to draw the attention of the Triads. And I don't care. My job is to get you to safety. You aren't safe here, so we're going to leave. Simple as that."

"Where am I supposed to go?"

"You'll come with me. I'll take you somewhere secure."

Oni swallowed down her usual sarcasm. The only thing she knew about this woman was that her mom said she'd keep her alive and not to mess with her.

"Okay," Oni began slowly. "I'm not in the best condition to leave."

"It will be taken care of. In the meantime, you will sign yourself out. I will have someone bring you a wheelchair. You'll sit in it, I'll wheel you out of here. Any questions?"

Oni could hear the impatience in Carla's voice, the distracted tone. Whatever this rescue was, it wasn't something Carla wanted to spend time doing. She had something else on her agenda and this was merely a pit stop along the way.

"Okay, okay," Oni repeated, doing her best to keep up with the ever-changing scenario, ignore the pain that had begun to throb in her side, and still shake off the remainder of the sedative. "My mom told me to trust you, so I do."

Carla gave a tight nod. "I'll return shortly." With movement like a lioness, she strode towards the door. Right before she opened it, Oni watched the woman's body posture change. She began to breathe heavier. Her shoulders raised. Her chest puffed out.

The door flung open. "Where's the doctor?" she demanded from the young guard. Once the door had closed behind her, Oni didn't hear anything else until it opened again.

"I can't stress enough that I don't think she's ready to be released, and this is definitely AMA...," the doctor said, trailing behind Carla, a clipboard with a release form in his hand.

"What a surprise? A doctor wants her to stay overnight, hike up those medical bills."

The doctor's face reddened. "Hey, now, that's not fair—"

"I'm not interested in *fair*," Carla continued. "My husband is a family practitioner, and my sister wants to leave. She'll be looked after. You've done your job, now let me get her out of this place where you and your staff let somebody *walk* in and try to hurt her." Carla put her hands on her hips and tapped her foot on the floor.

The doctor just stood there, mouth agape.

"That's what I thought," Carla finished. She took the clipboard and moved over to Oni. "Just sign right here, sweetie, and we'll get you back to my house. Your mom will be happier knowing that Alan is looking after you."

Oni could barely restrain the smile on her lips. This woman was *incredible*! She quickly signed the form and Carla ushered the doctor from the room.

"Don't worry, I'll help her get dressed. You," she said, pointing to the guard. Her body shifted again, this time with a hip popped out and her head slightly tilted. Oni had thought the woman beautiful before, but suddenly it was as if all eyes were drawn to her.

"I'm sorry for being like that before. Would you mind grabbing us a wheelchair so I can take her out to the car?" Carla asked the guard, her voice subtly full of honey.

The young guard flushed. "Uh, yeah, of course. It'd be my

pleasure."

"Thanks!" Carla gushed. She closed the door, turned, and became her professional self once more.

"Wow," Oni said. "That was...just wow."

"I enjoy psychology, just like you. Learning how to shift towards what a person will respond to makes things much easier than a heavy hand."

The concept made sense to Oni. While dealing with clients, she often changed tactics, depending on their background or demeanor. She just hadn't expected to witness such a complete and effortless transition into a different type of person so quickly.

After getting dressed and being wheeled down to the car, Oni let out a deep exhale once in the front seat. Her side ached and she clutched the painkiller prescription tightly in her hand. She hoped they'd stop at a pharmacy to fill the prescription sooner rather than later, but figured they'd have to arrive at her apartment and settle her in first.

As they drove away, Oni let her mind drift a bit, zoning out for a moment or two. She'd been a fool with the way she'd acted towards her mother. First thing she needed to do was call her mom and apologize. It was *not* a call she looked forward to, but maybe knowing she was safe and sound would help avoid too much of an "I told you so" lecture.

Oni pulled out her phone.

"Nope," Carla said, taking it away. "No phone calls. Once we get to the hotel, we can decide the next step, but you can't call anyone and let them know what occurred."

"I was only going to call my mother," Oni said, her

edginess returning. "You know, the one who sent you in the first place."

Carla threw Oni a look. "From the looks of it, we are the same age, and yet you behave like a child. As of this moment, I'm going to treat you like one. You've played with fire and not only gotten burned, but the fire is stalking you until it kills you. You are *extremely* lucky your mother had me in her life to come help you. And why do you think a person who knows about the Triads, can impersonate others, can come in and get you discharged from a hospital with no questions asked—why she came to be in your mother's life?"

Oni swallowed, hard, as the information sifted through her mind. "You're a Triad agent?"

"Was," Carla said, turning onto a heavily trafficked road. "I left, like she did."

"For the same reason?"

"No. The Triad I worked for murdered my husband."

Oni watched Carla remove one hand from the wheel and twist the wedding band around on her left hand.

"I'm sorry," Oni said lamely. "But don't you see? That's why I did what I did! I had to tell the world about the Triads, to expose them."

Carla's jaw tightened and she glared at her passenger. "You did *what?*"

Oni withered under Carla's stare. "I-I run a website. It's under a fake corporate name. I post about possible agents, their potential locations, the cases they were involved in—all the information my mom gave me."

"Information I'm sure she gave you to keep you safe, not

open your big mouth!"

Anger reared up inside Oni. "Now wait a minute—"

"What do you think happens now?" Carla interrupted, taking a corner a little tightly. The tires squealed through the turn. "Do you think you can return to your little website-creating life? You are *done*, Oni. *Terminada.* Once you are stable and manage on your own, your life is over. Forfeit."

Oni's forehead wrinkled. "Wait...like...like witness protection? New identity and all that?"

"Yes. But continually on the run. Individuals in government-run protection programs can try to make new lives somewhere. You won't get that luxury. The Triad women *are* everywhere. You'll have to keep on the move, every six months to a year, I'd say. More often in the beginning."

Oni's chest tightened. "No, wait, no, that can't be..." She couldn't breathe.

Carla casually hit a button and rolled down Oni's window a little. The cool dusk air hit her face like new life. She took in deep breaths, forcing herself not to think about her now blank future full of running and hiding.

"This is the world your mother was part of," Carla said, her tone softer. "The world *I* was part of. This is why we fought so hard to get out, why she gave you that information, to keep you one step ahead of the agents. It will take time to adjust, but you *can* do it. And you will have your mother's guidance to help, plus her knowledge of your true identity. It will keep you grounded. And that is more than most get in your situation."

Tears formed in the corners of Oni's eyes, but she refused to let them fall. She'd never withdrawn from a challenge her whole life. This could just be another challenge. Right?

Clearing her throat and wiping the moisture from her eyes, Oni registered that they were pulling into the hotel parking lot. "Yeah, you said hotel, but what about my apartment? I have to go there. All my things?"

"You will get a new place, new things."

Oni shook her head. "I'm diabetic. I need my insulin."

A tiny sigh. "You can't go there ever again. It is likely that Triad agents will have already been dispatched to your apartment to wait for you to return from the hospital."

"That won't matter if I die from insulin shock."

Carla pulled into a spot. She turned off the car and paused. "Insulin can be procured, but it will take a while..." She let out a longer sigh. "I will get you settled in the room then go to your apartment. I'll retrieve your medicine."

"What if someone's waiting there for me?"

A darkness entered Carla's eyes, which matched her tone. "I'll retrieve your medicine," she repeated.

29

October 19th
5:30 p.m.

Sean parked his Jag in a hospital guest parking spot and jogged to the lobby.

"I'm here to see a young woman, Oni," he said to the information desk. "She was just admitted today with a stab wound."

The nurse looked up and smiled broadly. "I'm sorry," he said, his large hazel eyes bright. "But visiting hours are over for the day."

Sean removed his badge from his belt and held it up.

"Oh," the nurse said, his huge smile fading fast. "Of course. Let me just look up the room…"

"No need. I was here earlier. I know the way." Sean moved through the corridors with confidence. When he arrived, the first thing he noticed was that the young guard no longer remained stationed at the door and the door itself stood open.

Sean popped his head in.

The bed sat empty.

Oh God, he thought. *This "Carla" woman already got here, and Oni is dead.* Adrenaline shot through him, and he crossed over to the nearest nurses' station.

"Excuse me," he said, his heart pounding. "Where is the young woman who was in this room. Her name is Oni." He held up his badge.

"Uh..." the nurse said, looking up the information on the computer. Freckles popped out against her pale skin. "She...she checked out. About fifteen minutes ago."

"Checked...checked out? But she'd been stabbed in the side."

"Sorry, sir. That's all the information I have. She signed a release form."

"Do you have her home address? I have reason to believe she's in danger."

The nurse's eyes widened. "Oh, uh, yes, yes right here." She scribbled it down on a pad of paper and handed him the top sheet.

"Thank you," he said. Turning on his heel, he navigated the less crowded hallways, headed towards his car, and took off after programming the address into his GPS. Traffic had picked up, but he still made it to the location in under twenty minutes.

Sean parked, turned off his car, grabbed his weapon, and

put his hand on the door handle of the car.

He froze.

The address. He recognized it. This was the address of the Roswall Corporation—the very place he'd been heading to all this time.

Oni must be the one responsible for the website which revealed names of Triad agents.

That's why they went after her.

But this "Carla" woman sent to help Oni... Was she friend or foe? If she really *was* the same Carla that had taken Charlotte from Mae and the Coalition group, and at this point there was too much coincidence to believe otherwise, then she may know the whereabouts of Charlotte as well.

Or worse, may be responsible for Charlotte's death.

Sean's chest rose and fell. Feelings of fury mixed with helplessness churned inside him. Charlotte had wanted to tell him, but he understood why she'd resisted. He hadn't told her either about he and Elaine reinvestigating the Triads. After all the "Messiah" talk and Charlotte's near-death experience, he hadn't wanted her to ever deal with those women again.

So, Charlotte had done the same thing—kept Sean shielded from the truth to protect him.

If—no, *when*—he found Charlotte, he promised no more secrets. He'd tried to protect her, and she'd tried to protect him, and they were still *both* wrapped up in all this Triad business.

No more. Determination filling him, Sean pulled at the door handle and exited the car. He ran up the steps to the building and was about to buzz the correct apartment number, but before he could, the outside door swung open. Sean thought about sneaking in behind the person once they departed when he glanced up into their face.

The therapist who had counseled him after he'd been shot returned his gaze.

Carla.

Sean blinked.

Carla. Fucking CARLA!

"What the—?"

Before he could think she'd already shoved him through the door. A flurry of movements and a hit to his elbow area caused the bottom half of his right arm to go numb, at the same time he'd been reaching for his weapon. He held up his left arm in defense, but she came at him with extended fingers, swooping underneath his extended arm, and poking him roughly in the lower back. His legs collapsed underneath him.

"Stop!" he yelled, the feeling returning slowly to his legs, though they still tingled.

"Why couldn't you leave things *alone*?" she hissed at him.

Sean stared. How? How could his therapist be *the* Carla? The same one who'd taken Charlotte. The same one who'd helped him come to terms with the whole Triad situation in the first place. The same one who'd just gotten Oni out of the hospital and was now at the woman's apartment who *happened* to be the woman Sean had been searching for on this whole trip because of the Triad website she ran.

Sean's brain couldn't process everything fast enough. He had too many questions and the only thing that came out was, "You're under arrest."

Carla tilted her head. She still held the same analyzing facial expression, as if this was nothing more than another session. "For what?"

Sean guffawed. "For what? For...for everything! Impersonating a psychologist. Being involved with the Triads. Kidnapping Charlotte. Taking Oni from the hospital and then breaking into her building." He paused to catch a breath. "And where is Charlotte? You better not have hurt her..."

Carla glanced at him on the floor and sighed. He hated the feeling of being a kid throwing a tantrum while an adult rolled their eyes.

"Detective...Sean," she began again, this time her tone softer. "You know a lot more than I thought you would, but you're mistaken on every count. I didn't impersonate anyone. I *am* a licensed psychologist. I *was* involved with the Triads, but now I'm working to take them down. I didn't kidnap Charlotte, I rescued her from captivity. She is safe and unharmed. That's all I can say about that situation for now. And as for Oni, I accompanied her as she checked herself out of the hospital on the wishes of her mother to get her to a safe location. As you well know, she was attacked by Triad agents today. I thought she'd be safer somewhere else."

Sean just stood there. The words rolled around inside his brain. Part of him rejoiced that Charlotte was still alive and well, but the other continued to seethe with rage. This woman was trying to talk her way out of the situation. And yet...and yet...He tried to think of a way to make Carla the villain, but everything she said made sense. "But...you've killed people," he said lamely.

"Yes. Some were innocent. Those, I can't undo. Some to stop others from being killed. Those I'd do again. But, as you well know, there is no proof of these deeds. Your laws can't hold me. And if you go through with this, you'll put other lives in danger. There are still threats out there the authorities can't stop."

Sean's body began to recover from the numbing blows, and he slowly rose to a standing position. "You're talking about the other Triads. And the arsonist group."

Carla nodded. "I am working to prevent them from continuing their work, but there have been a few...hiccups along the way." She crossed her arms. "Can I ask what *you're* doing here?"

"No," he said, the anger returning. "You lied. You deceived me and my colleagues. You manipulated us. Why should I answer any of your questions?"

"Because I could kill you right now and no one would ever know who did it. But I'm not going to do that because the truth is...I need help."

Sean had *not* expected that response. "Help? You? Aren't you and your Triads all-powerful or whatever."

She pursed her lips. "I am not part of a Triad anymore. My resources have...there have been complications. And...honestly, it was not my idea to ask for your help. But seeing how resourceful you can be, I can understand why you may be useful."

"Oh thanks, I think."

Carla loosened her stance, arms hanging at her sides. Sean had no illusion that she couldn't strike him again just as fast as before, but she seemed at least to be less tense.

"What do you say to a truce?" she suggested. "At this point, my options are limited. I believe I can shed light on the holes in your theories and you could provide me the knowledge regarding how you learned about Oni."

"I didn't know who she was in the hospital," he said. "I came here following her website. The incident in the café was a complete accident."

Carla began to laugh.

"What's so funny?"

"That *maldito* website," she cursed. "She is more visible than she thought."

"Aren't you here because of it?"

"No. But I think the agents who went after her were."

Sean paused, still thinking about pulling his weapon, but she was *very* fast. He didn't know if he could do it before she...well whatever she did to make him go limp. "Are you going to run away or kick my ass or something if I let my guard down?"

"Not if you agree to a truce. I know you to be a truthful person. I'll take you at your word."

"And now I know you to be a liar so how can I believe you?"

"Because I have Oni. You can ask her any questions you'd like." She waited a beat. "It is the only way to advance, for both of us. Otherwise, I will leave and you won't find me again."

"I found you this time."

"You weren't looking for me. You wanted Oni, who I have access to. You won't find her again, either, after this, because she'll be under my protection."

Sean thought it over. Actually, at this point, if Oni no longer stayed at this address, then his trip was over. She was right. He couldn't move forward without Carla's assistance. And, it seemed, she couldn't move forward without his.

Sean wondered about Woods and Elaine, what they might do or how they might think in this same situation. He had a feeling Elaine would jump at the chance. As much as this stuff scared her, her journalistic instincts would want her to learn as much information as possible. Although, she'd seemed more and more cautious lately. Still, who better than an actual Triad source for details?

Woods, on the other hand, played it a little more by the book. He may not be too keen on working with a killer. Except, at this point, he may do anything for a lead to the arson group and since Oni had posted Mae's name, she had a connection to the Triads he could learn more about.

Besides, this was the only way he could find out about Charlotte's location.

With a deep exhale, Sean held out his hand. "Truce."

30

October 19th

6:00 p.m.

Anxiety flooded through Mae. She had no desire to have this meeting. Avoiding everyone in the Coalition group, even Patrick, hadn't been easy, but eventually, she knew she couldn't outrun them forever.

It wasn't as if she'd lost Charlotte on her watch—hell, the guards had already paid for that with their lives—but she'd been there. On site. Fought with Carla and lost. Lost Charlotte. Lost what they needed for their final step.

The truth was, Mae being there at all that night proved to be an anomaly. So, the question of this meeting had to be: why had she been there in the first place?

That question deserved an answer, but Mae didn't want to give a truthful one. She'd been there with doubts, with questions for Charlotte. This entire operation and its inconsistencies gnawed at her brain like a termite into new house floorboards.

After she'd awakened that morning, something hadn't seemed right. First off, she hadn't woken up in quite the same place as where she'd been laying when she'd fought Carla. Instead, she was closer to the door, almost as if she'd left the room temporarily and then tried to return. But, since she'd blacked out, she couldn't be sure she hadn't regained consciousness, felt groggy, and been confused. Or perhaps Carla had moved her body while she'd been knocked out. Either way, the replacement guards who'd found her had a lot of questions.

They wanted to keep her on site until their leader returned, but Mae was excellent at talking her way out of situations.

"I have a job today," she'd told them. "You don't want me to miss an appointment, do you? We all know the consequences." The threat of delaying any part of their plan *and* Mae's high ranks in the Coalition got her released from too much suspicion.

"She'll want to see you when she gets back," one of the new guards said, tossing her long locks behind her. "She sounded pissed when we called her this morning."

"She's not the only one," Mae bluffed, heading for the door. "We've had a breach. It needs to be sealed up." She looked them over. "You know what to do here. Clean house. Create a plausible scenario for the bodies."

"Of course."

And just like that, Mae was in charge of the situation again.

Of course, she couldn't bluff her way through the meeting. Her boss was too smart for that.

She needed a cover story, so she'd taken most of the day to think of one. Problem was, each one sounded less feasible than the last.

Time crept closer to their scheduled meeting of 5:30 p.m. Mae paced. The sea air whipped at her short hair, causing it to flutter. Seagulls squawked in the distance, no doubt looking for one last meal before the sun set. Soft *dongs* of boat bells rung while the smell of fish and brine filled her nose on the dock.

I'm not going to get out of this, she thought, staring at the choppy water. Because the truth was, she *didn't* trust her boss anymore. Too many things didn't add up. Too much of what Charlotte had said crept through her mind that day, poisoning it. Or so she thought. What had actually happened was that the misgivings shifted from Charlotte onto her boss.

How can you doubt her? Mae asked herself as she continued to pace. *She meets all the criteria of the Messiah.*

So does Charlotte, her mind countered.

So, which one was the true Messiah if they both fit?

Mae heard footsteps. She turned, ready to meet her fate, her hand gripped around her favorite knife inside her jacket pocket, just in case things went south.

"Hello, Mae," her boss said, approaching. Her long, white wool coat, hugging her curves exactly right, made her look like a professional model who'd just come from a winter-themed shoot. The Italian woman's cheeks were rosy, but whether from the blustery wind or flushed with anger, Mae couldn't tell.

She'd find out soon enough.

"Hello, Isabella," Mae said, hoping the words sounded steadier than they felt. With a wave of her non-knife-holding hand she gestured to their surroundings. "Strange place to meet."

"I'm expecting a shipment. Fresh supplies."

Mae merely nodded.

"Why were you there?" Isabella asked.

Straight to it.

Mae's genius mind, who'd hacked complex computer codes and databases, had no idea what story Isabella might believe.

So, she decided to start with the truth.

"I had doubts."

The tiniest of wrinkles formed upon Isabella's brow. "Doubts?"

"Yeah. Charlotte was...convincing."

"But you know she would say anything to survive. Unease amongst the ranks...it's a classic tactic."

"I know."

A slight pause. "But you still believed her." The question came as a statement.

Mae shook her head, a plausible lie forming in her mind. "No. She had some valid points. I wanted to further interrogate her. Away from prying eyes."

Isabella clasped her hands in front of her. "And whose eyes would have been 'prying?' Do you not trust the others in your

Coalition group?"

Mae straightened. "I know you have had to...restrain me in the past during interrogations. I didn't want anyone to know how I questioned her. That was wrong of me." A smaller admission of guilt would result in a less severe punishment.

"But if you didn't believe her, why ask her anything at all? Why listen to her in the first place?"

"I wanted to check for holes in the plan and I didn't want others to know about those holes. If Charlotte found weaknesses, they needed to be sealed up." Mae waited while Isabella stood there. She hated lying, but it was the only way to save her skin. She'd been foolish to ever question Isabella as the true Messiah. Looking at her now in her long, flowing coat, she appeared like a glowing white goddess.

"I'm...I'm sorry," Mae continued.

Finally, Isabella spoke. "Do you still have doubts?"

"No," Mae said. But a part of her didn't really believe that. Foolish or not, Charlotte had made a valid point. Why had Isabella connected the Coalition to a fake Messiah? The only reason to do so was to set them up for a fall once Isabella claimed herself as the true Messiah.

But why? How could Isabella keep using the Coalition if they appeared to be attached to the villain? Especially once Charlotte was dead. There'd be no reason for the Coalition to do anything anymore.

Maybe she just won't call us the Coalition, but we'll still help her.

It was a possibility, but then why hadn't Isabella told them any of this? For all Mae and the others knew, they'd planned to continue to go after thirds and Triads who didn't follow Isabella.

Except...except that was if they didn't follow Charlotte, not Isabella. Isabella planned to show herself as opposite to a tyrant.

Mae hated these thoughts, missing the clarity of the kill, but they came anyway, bombarding her as she stood there, waiting for Isabella to accept her lie or not.

A different feeling began to steal over her. A sense of resistance. Here Isabella stood, the perfect representation of the Messiah, and yet...and yet...

The Messiah was supposed to represent truth, symbolize openness. Isabella worked in the shadows, setting up Charlotte to take the fall. She'd helped Charlotte every step of the way, convinced her to be the Messiah in the first place, just so she could be seen as a fake. Yes, Mae was a killer, even enjoyed killing, but she did it for a reason—a belief.

Charlotte made her question.

Isabella expected obedience.

Which one represented a tyrant after all?

Isabella must have recognized the shift in Mae because she gave a tiny smile.

"I've lost you, haven't I?" she said, her tone full of sadness.

"You aren't the Messiah, are you?" Mae countered.

Isabella's tone didn't change, though it chilled Mae to the core of her being. "Why not? I fit the criteria. Born with a mark that faded to reveal my true perfection, isolated from those around me because of my intelligence, and one with death, as comfortable with it as life itself." She paused. "On top of that, the Triads already sought me out. I *fit* within the Triads. Charlotte didn't want to have anything to do with us. She believes we are a bunch of lowlife killers who decide the fate of innocents on a whim."

Mae couldn't be certain if Isabella was really trying to convince her or herself.

"Maybe," Mae said, gripping her knife a bit harder. "But maybe that's the kind of Messiah the Triads need. If we are willing to follow someone who doesn't question everything we do, who doesn't evolve, then aren't we exactly the problem the Book talks about?"

Isabella's face didn't change. She just looked...sad. "I hoped this wouldn't happen," she said, "but the truth is, this will be much easier if you're against me."

Thwick.

Pain tore next to her shoulder blade and into her chest, like a burning hot ball of fire tearing through cotton.

Mae opened her jacket and peered down. Blood pooled across her shirt.

"It didn't come out," she said about the bullet. Her knees buckled and she fell onto the damp dock.

Isabella stood over her, waving past her to someone behind Mae.

A shooter, Mae managed to think. She could barely put together any other thoughts as all her functionality seemed to focus on the searing pain in her sternum.

Isabella stared downwards. "You had to go, of course. I can't have psychopaths on my team. As the Messiah, it's my duty to get us back on track. Insanity has no place within the

Triads. No mental imperfections. We will only kill because we must and only because we know there is no other way. Not because something inside is broken."

Isabella placed a heeled boot alongside Mae's body.

Mae could do nothing but attempt to breathe through the fluid filling her lungs. The sky seemed so dark for some reason, but she was sure the sun hadn't fully set yet. *Where are the stars?* she thought.

"I'm glad you turned against me," Isabella said softly. "This would have been so much harder if you'd been devoted to me when I had you killed."

With a shove, Mae's body flipped over and fell off the side of the dock. Right before she plunged into the icy water, she saw a person on the boat who'd been behind her.

The shooter.

Patrick.

Her love.

The boat exploded.

Patrick exploded with it.

Then the world disappeared.

Mags felt lighting flash through her entire body.

"Come on!" she heard someone call out.

Dry lips with fishy breath covered her mouth, plunging air into her, filling her lungs.

"Okay, get back!"

Once more, lightning hit her.

"Okay stop! She has a pulse."

Mags' eyelids flew open, and she gulped in a giant breath.

Air filled her body. Then, the pain set in. Her whole body felt cold and numb except for an explosion of fire in her back and within her chest.

"Hang on, little lady," the first man said. "Ambulance is on its way."

"She's losing blood," another one said.

"Flip her over. Gotta get pressure on it."

Grayness swam before her.

She was alive.

She remembered dying.

But she was alive.

And she was Mags.

"Never thought I'd need to use that thing!" the first man said. Mags, with her head lying flat against a wet, wooden surface, saw a bright yellow box next to her with dials.

Defibrillator. Her brain registered the word, then realized the truth. She really *had* died.

"Well, she ain't out of the woods yet. Good thing she fell into the water after that explosion. Probably kept her cold enough. Now, here, keep that pressure on. I'm gonna get her something from the bait shop to keep her warm. Teddy always has like six coats anyway."

The pain intensified as something pressed against her back and Mags felt like she might pass out at any moment.

I might become Mae again if I do that!

Concentrating on the pain, she used it to keep herself awake, to stay focused. She stared at a knot in the dock beneath her, drawing in one breath after another. The pain was unreal.

I might die. For real. I have to...

"I need a phone," she said out loud, her teeth chattering.

"Sweetheart, just stay calm. Someone's coming real soon to patch you up."

"Phone!" she demanded. The energy used made her head spin. She smashed a hand on the dock, using it to regain her focus.

With an exasperated-sounding exhale, the man handed her the phone. She dialed the precinct. "Forward me to Detective Trann, please," she said, trying to keep her voice steady.

"Is she a cop?" one of the men asked.

The waves knocked against the underside of the dock, spitting up bits of salty water into her face. It was strange, now, at the end, the little things she noticed.

The water tasted of life.

The air smelled of sadness.

The world never seemed so big and so small at the same time.

Click. The line changed over to Sean's phone.

Ring....

"Please..." she whispered.

Ring...

"Sean, I need you...pick up..."

Ring...

31

October 19th
6:15 p.m.

Sean drove behind Carla's car, still not quite believing the situation. A strange fog hung around some of the light posts, creating an ill-at-ease feeling that matched his own.

This had been his therapist, for God's sake. A woman he'd confided in about his past, his present, even his future. He'd told her so many personal things, things he'd never shared with anyone else.

And she turned out to be a con artist who had lied, manipulated, and killed.

Still, she was the best chance he had of finally being able to find Charlotte, bring down the Triads, and get his life back.

Get *everyone's* life back.

On the twenty-minute drive to the hotel, Sean decided to finally check in with Woods and Elaine. There was no use putting it off until the next day because, frankly, he had no idea what might occur from this point forward.

Sean called Elaine first, knowing she'd probably be upset if he didn't.

"I was *just* about to call you," she gushed. "I've been getting worried. I mean, I didn't want to interrupt in case you were interrogating someone or something, but I mean it's been a few hours since you were supposed to have gotten to the Philly area so I—"

"Elaine," he interrupted. "I'm fine. I don't have a lot of time. I'm following up on a lead, but I wanted to make sure things were okay on your end first. How were your interviews?"

"Dead end. Literally," she said. He could almost *hear* her flipping her hair to one side.

Sean frowned. "What do you mean?"

"The bunker women? All dead."

Several moments of shocked silence passed. "Wait, *all* of them? Weren't there like six women?"

"Seven. Get this. A *fire* broke out in their minimum-security prison. No one else was harmed. All seven of them were burned to a crisp. I checked in with the coroner on the case. She told me they'd been *sedated* before the fire started."

"Holy crap," he said, smoothly taking a turn to follow Carla's car. These fires were getting out of control, becoming more public, and the body count was definitely adding up.

"You know, I've been told countless times now about how

these women mean business, how they cover their tracks, how they can get to anyone, anywhere. It honestly didn't sink in until now." She cleared her throat. "Which, uh, leads me to what I wanted to talk to you about."

"Is it important? It's just I only have about ten minutes and I still want to check in with Woods."

Her voice pitched higher. "It won't take long. And Woods is fine. He spoke to me a couple hours ago. He's staying overnight and has an appointment with Zack in the morning. Kid thinks it's an interview for a paper."

"All right, so what do you want to tell me?"

"I, uh..." she started. He'd never heard her so hesitant before.

"What's up?" Sean asked, concern building.

"I think I'm going to back out. Of this whole thing. The Triad thing I mean."

Sean didn't register what she'd said for a few moments. "Wait, are you serious?"

"Deadly. Pun intended. Look, you convinced me to stay in this when Gloria was killed—"

"Now wait a minute," he said, talking over her, "I didn't—"

She continued, speaking louder. "But this has gone too far. Too many people have now died and to be honest, I don't see this ever ending. There are too many Triads and they are going to find me sooner or later. I want to go back to my life. I want to report stories about fires that are just fires. It's too much. I'm sorry."

She hung up.

Sean stared at the phone in its dashboard holder, listening

to the sound of silence.

He couldn't believe it. After everything they'd all been through, she was quitting, just like that.

She's not in law enforcement. She's not equipped to handle this sort of thing. Cut her some slack.

Still, it felt like a slap to the face. He realized in that moment that *Elaine* had been the one to suck him once again into all this Triad stuff. *He'd* been done with it, and she'd come in with her theories and coincidences. And now she wanted out.

But the anger didn't really come from her wanting to bail while she still could, it was that the face of his group had completely changed. Instead of Tay, Wilt, Mags, Millan, and Charlotte as his team, he had an Interpol officer from London, an ex-Triad agent, and a Triad-related website owner. It was as if these women had sliced apart his existence, leaving him with rifts between himself and the people in his real life, instead creating tenuous webs between himself and these new participants of this Triad life.

Even though Elaine had been a more recent addition, she'd been there from the beginning of this new rabbit hole. He'd come to count on the fact that whatever crazy notion or idea he had, he could go to her with it, and she'd be willing to check it out. He'd started to depend on her being there, on her friendship, and on her willingness to listen.

Just like Juliette.

Just like Mags.

Just like Charlotte.

Another one, gone.

The hotel glowed in the distance, like a beacon of light

guiding him into a murkier path of self-destruction.

Suddenly, Sean felt extremely tired as he pulled into a parking spot. Hope sucked away from him like a vampire feeding. What could he possibly do to stop these women and not get everyone around him killed, including himself?

Carla exited her vehicle and motioned for him to join her.

Sean simply sat. Inside was a woman who could give him answers, who could pull him further in. But was Elaine right?

When was enough, enough?

Carla approached the driver's window. He rolled it down a crack.

"Problem?" she asked.

Sean kept staring at the hotel, its randomly lit and darkened rooms like blacked out or missing teeth.

Like a fun house, Sean thought, remembering a circus he went to when he'd been young. Except once he'd gotten inside, he hadn't enjoyed it. The rooms were different sizes, odd angles, strange paint patterns to make you dizzy and unsteady.

Would this place treat him the same way? Would he continue to feel off balance until he finally fell?

"Sean," she said. "We have to go. Oni will need medical attention."

With automatic movements, Sean opened and closed the door, then locked it behind him. He followed Carla inside, into the elevator, and up to the fifth floor. The doors all looked the same, passing him without any meaning. Did any of their occupants know what was going on right down the hall? Would it only get them killed if they did?

Carla approached room 514, slid her card into the slot,

and it turned green. She opened the door a notch, but paused, turning towards him.

"There is something you should know before we go—"

Sean's phone rang, cutting her off.

Probably Elaine, wanting to explain more.

It rang again.

I really don't feel like talking to her.

A third ring.

"Do you want to answer that?" Carla asked.

He pulled it from his pocket. It was a number he didn't recognize. Normally he didn't answer unknown numbers, but at this moment hearing something normal like a spammy call about changing his car insurance made him ache inside.

He nodded to Carla that she could keep entering the room.

"Sean?" the voice said over the phone.

It took half a second to realize who he was hearing.

"Mags?" he said with disbelief. He stopped in the doorway, shock freezing him still.

"I don't have much time," she wheezed. "I've been shot."

Suddenly, another voice wafted through the open entrance to the room. The sound swirled around him.

He knew that voice.

"Sean, are you there?" Mags asked on the other end.

"I'm here..." he said, trailing off.

"Isabella is in charge of the Coalition. She's setting up Charlotte."

Siren noises filled the background of the phone call. Then, dead silence.

"Mags?" he said into the receiver. *Did she say...Isabella?* "Mags, are you there?"

The other voice sounded again in the hotel room. "Carla, good. I did what I could for Oni."

I know that voice...

He finished entering the room. The world stopped.

There she stood.

Charlotte.

ABOUT THE AUTHOR

Christa has also moved into the world of detective fiction with her international bestselling novel, SPIDER'S TRUTH, the first in the *Detective Trann series.*

Looking for something Young Adult? Try the YA fantasy *Land of Iyah* trilogy, starting with book 1: THE JADE CASTLE.

Aside from her novels, Christa has also authored a graphic novel, HOLLOW, and 6-issue follow-up comic book series HOLLOW'S PRISM from Green-Eyed Unicorn Comics. (with illustrator Conrad Teves.)

Originally from Milwaukee, WI, Christa was exposed to many different things through her education, including an elementary Spanish immersion program, a vocal/opera program in high school, and her eventual B.S. in Biology. Her love of entomology and marine biology helped while writing her science fiction/fantasy aliens/creatures.

As for why she writes, Christa had this to say: "I write because I have a story that needs to come out. I write because I can't NOT write. I write because I love creating something that pulls me out of my own world and lets me for a little while get lost inside someone or someplace else. And I write because I HAVE to know how the story ends."

You can find more about Christa and her other books at:
www.ChristaYelichKoth.com